Hit by the Dealer

written by
E. Craig McKay

published by

HALL BROTHERS
ENTERTAINMENT

Background for Hit by the Dealer was drawn from my shooting competitions and poker games throughout United States, Spain and Canada. Special thanks to Pinecrest Revolver & Gun Club of St. Catharines. Bruce Tallon, Ray Matthews, Bob Button, and Bill Morrissey provided valued input and critiques of drafts. More credit is due than I can ever express to my wife, JoAnne Gambarotto-McKay, for endless hours of proofreading and editing and for her constant support.

Prologue

Carl was dead; that was certain. But why?

Had he taken his own life? If he had, was it to protect her? Could someone have killed him? Who would do that?

Joyce looked at the flowers and card of condolence from Mr. Rizzo.

Mr. Rizzo, it all changed with him, him and the land.

People at the office said Rizzo looked like a mobster. Could that be true? He seemed so proper. Even if he was, how could that connect with Carl? Carl was a business consultant.

Carl was dead; nothing else seemed to matter.

The title phrase of the song "Is That All There Is?" kept repeating like a 'mind worm.' Twenty-five years together. Is that all you get? Is that all there is?

Now there was nothing.

Chapter 1

Texas Hold'em

A version of Poker in which each player gets two cards down and shares five common cards to make the best five-card poker hand.

"So, who won last week?" Carl asked, as he set a bottle of Bud Light on the side table and settled into his seat at the poker table. His eyes slid across Tom, Dave, Terry and Russell and focused upon Darren, who he had already heard had been the last one standing (or sitting actually, he corrected himself) the previous Tuesday.

The men had been playing this weekly game for two years now, just the six of them. Once in a while Tom's twin brother, Robert (not Bob, Robert), would be in town and join in. Five of the fellows lived in Queenston and Carl was nearby. Robert lived in the family home in Hamilton.

"Darren won again," Terry said. "He drew to an inside straight to win the last hand."

"That makes twice he's won in the last three weeks," Tom volunteered.

"Yep, and he was second the other week," Dave added. "The boy wants watching."

Dave was the statistician, and the one Carl watched most closely. He played the odds well. You would never catch Dave drawing to an inside straight, and seldom betting on a hand that was not already pretty solid. Darren was the one to chase hands. That was why he usually lost.

"I think those are the only two weeks I've won this year," Darren chipped in. "But I'm planning to continue the streak." Darren and Terry were the youngest of the group at 40. Only Dave, at 47 was older than Carl who had turned 46 on June 10, three months ago, exactly two weeks before his wife Joyce. The group was pretty well the same age even though they had met here in the neighborhood rather than by being school mates.

Just keep chasing with bad hands, Carl thought. In fact no one took the game too seriously. They took turns hosting it and each put in twenty bucks which got split 100 to first and 20 to second when they had their usual six players and 100 / 40 when they occasionally had seven. The past week Carl had been out of town on business, so the five others had played and split up the pot 80/20.

It was a friendly game where no one won much or lost much. Social poker.

Carl traveled from time to time. He never discussed where he went. Mostly he just didn't mention it. If asked, he always said he was in New York, the place where he had been born and grown up. Ask him anything about NYNY and he knew it. No one asked much anymore. They'd got used to the fact that Carl didn't want to talk shop.

Chapter 2

Play tight

"Tight" describes a player who plays cautiously; "Loose" the opposite.

Carl was the unnoticed business traveler. Home Land Security wasn't interested in casual calls home from people like him. Even his occasional call to Bermuda or Spain was either to a bank, or business agent, or one of the corporations Carl was associated with as part of his work. The subject of the calls was about contracts and paying bills and making investments. It would bore anyone overhearing them.

From time to time his home life brought him into contact with the people his wife worked with in real estate. They were usually pleasant, charming people whose main interest in life was to sell houses. His personal social circle was from his present neighborhood and came from a variety of jobs and professions. Mostly they talked amongst themselves about sports, politics, music, and other trivia. Some of the guys would talk, or more likely complain, about work from time to time. Carl was a good listener. You learn more by listening than talking.

Carl had made it his business to know everything about what the other people did. He knew where they had gone to school, where they had grown up, and where they worked. He knew the same about their wives. They would be surprised just how much he knew about them; he never discussed himself and never let on that he knew or cared anything about their lives beyond casual politeness.

If asked what line of work he was in, Carl always described it as consulting and never became more specific than to say business consulting. If pressed he would explain that insider trading information rules and trade secrets made it necessary for him not to discuss his clients.

Years ago he had realized that no one ever seems to know what a business consultant did. It provided a perfect cover for his actual work as a hit man.

With the small, unmatched, off-suit cards he was getting as his down pairs, Carl was not being tempted to call many hands. When he was small or big blind, he stayed in with anything as long as no one more than doubled the blind. Tonight he had no hands which encouraged any major commitment, so he just let the play flow by while watching his fellow players for tells or predictable reactions which helped guess as to what they probably held.

Tom was getting off to a good start and was building up his stack at the expense of Terry and Russ. Both were impatient players who were unwilling, perhaps unable, to wait for good cards to come. They almost always were knocked out early;

even when they had cards which were above average, they didn't finish well.

It is hard to lose with a really good hand, but if you don't vary your betting patterns you tend to win smaller pots because you chase others out. They were both fairly predictable as well about what they called with and bet on.

Sometimes it is best to underplay your hand, and sometimes you have to bet as if you can't be beat. But, if you bet only when you've got the goods, you can't expect others to call you. As with most activities, including contractual killing, you need to be a bit unpredictable in your approach.

You certainly had to know when to throw a hand away despite how big the pot was. You also had to know when the risk was too great to attempt a take out.

His recent trip to Florida was an example of that.

Tells, such as holding the cards closer to you when they were good, or looking at your cards after the flop could give away a lot. Appearance and behavior were equally important in the activity by which Carl made his living. There, however, the stakes were higher.

Chapter 3

According to Hoyle

Hoyle, the best known authority of card rules and procedures.

Carl looked like a business man. His hair was brown, touched now with shadings of grey. His eyes were pale and either grey-blue or blue-grey depending on the light. He behaved like a conservative worker bee, busy but not clearly doing any one thing. He put effort into seeming ordinary. His was the face you saw three or four times a day and didn't realize you'd seen it more than once. Better yet, didn't ever really see it.

He bought suits that were just on the edge of being out of style and middle of the road, off-the-rack looking. If he required casual clothes he bought them where he was working, ran them through a couple cycles in a Laundromat before wearing them, and threw them away before he came home. He simply put them in a green garbage bag and slipped them into a Goodwill or Salvation Army bin.

Specific skills and a special personality were required to do his job. He knew how to use his tools with precision and accuracy and he didn't share confidences. He was careful. He stuck to the rules he had developed and never took chances unless there was no better way.

A pair of Queens were dealt to him and Carl made a small bet. No one called him and Carl made a point of showing the pair. It was sometimes useful to create the impression that you were only betting on good cards to set up a bluff later. Other times he would flip over the useless cards he had bluffed with, or make a show of burying them in the slough pile as if they had been really good. Letting people think they could predict your cards and betting could allow you to mislead them later.

When working on a hit, Carl would prefer not to be noticed at all. If things went well the target would never know what hit him and no one else would know he was dead until someone stumbled over the body. Carl did not handle removals; body moving was not in his job description. He also did not use garrotes, saps, bombs, or rifles. There were some who used those tools, but Carl was a specialist. He used only hand guns and those discretely at close range.

Carl liked his job. He only worked when he wanted to and only a few weeks per year.

The pay was good. The work was interesting and varied. He worked without supervision. No one evaluated the quality of his performance as long as the target was dead and he wasn't caught. He paid no professional fees or union dues. The retirement plan was very flexible.

He had an office set up at home and spent several hours a day working on spreadsheets and doing research. His wife, Joyce, assumed that the time he spent working was related to his business. It was. She had her own work as a real estate agent, so their time was flexible but often chaotic. By choice they had no children, so the lack of a regular routine presented no problem to either of them.

Probably what he did wasn't much different to what an actual business consultant would do. He invested his own money carefully. Carl kept abreast of industrial and economic trends and all types of investments. As in most other things he did, he preferred high quality investments with little risk and reasonable returns.

He had noticed that in poker the same approach worked well. You didn't have to win a lot on any one hand, you just had to win more than you lost and more often.

Joyce was used to the fact that he read business reviews, spent three or four hours per day in his office working on the computer, referencing the Internet for financial news and economic information. Except for what he did on "business trips," Carl didn't have to keep any secrets. He never had to worry about anyone finding what was on the computer or which sites he visited on the Net. It was all anyone might expect from someone who was staying informed about business and the economy. Hell, he probably could be a business consultant, he often thought.

What he was actually doing during the hours spent in his office was directing his own investments. If he said so himself, he was pretty good at it. Perhaps some day he would hang up a shingle and become a professional financial adviser. From what he had seen it wasn't rocket science, just good research and common sense.

That might come if he retired from his primary occupation. For the moment he had enough to keep him focused. He had reasonable financial goals which he had pretty much achieved. He was careful and wanted to stay healthy to enjoy retirement.

Retirement was an important consideration in any occupation. Carl had a self directed plan which seemed pretty good to him. It was also part of his personal security.

Clearly one of the potential problems with his occupation was that a killing might be traced back to him. To avoid that, he had set up a simple, yet effective way of distancing himself completely.

The money could not be traced to him.

He was paid a fee for services. That fee was paid by his agent, Stan, into an offshore bank account which was a corporate account. That account paid monies into two other similar accounts at other banks. One of those was his secret, off-shore retirement account and he made sure that money was diversified into real estate in several countries and secure bonds in various currencies. The other account paid Carl a regular consulting fee which he faithfully reported as income and paid tax on. Some of that went into legitimate onshore investments.

The level of his official income was reasonable and he lived within that income. He did nothing to attract undue attention. The corporation which he controlled and which paid him had also set up a perfectly legitimate life annuity fund which he could activate anytime he cared to, or would go to Joyce if he died. Things happen.

His finances read like an open book and he came across as highly respectable. You can do anything you want as long as you pay taxes on it.

He was content to know that he already had enough in his retirement fund to quit any time he wanted to.

No one who paid for his professional services knew where he lived or his real name. It actually worked well for them too because he had no idea who was actually paying for any hit. They couldn't turn him in, and, if caught, he couldn't say who they were.

Carl never met people he received a contract from, and had only brief and final contact with the subjects of the contract. Carl had a business agent who represented others like himself. He had met Stan a little over twenty-five years ago and their contact since then had been by telephone and more and more lately by Internet.

While away, he called home frequently, but he either used Skype or a throw away phone. Computers could be anywhere. Both they and phones could be tracked if you really attracted attention. Carl didn't. If he called on business, for example to Stan in New York, he used a public phone or a cell phone reserved for that, and if prudent discarded it. It was a cost of doing business.

In Europe mobile telephones have to be registered, but in America throw away phones and unregistered guns are readily available. In Canada the guns are a bit more difficult to obtain, but the border is very close.

Carl wondered if either he or Stan would even recognize one another if they passed in the street. He hoped not. Stan probably didn't even know that he now lived in Canada under the name Carl Hill.

In the movies the bad guys can never go straight. "You're part of the mob, Rocky. You can't get out." In reality Carl could drop out by just breaking contact with Stan.

Someday Stan would stop contacting him or he'd send one last Hasta la vista message to Stan and disappear. He wouldn't have to get out of town either. He could stay where he was or move somewhere else as he liked.

He was already straight, if you didn't count the bodies.

Unlike the characters in the stories, Carl did not have a public reputation. No young gunslinger would hunt him down to put a notch on his gun.

He had no guilty conscience.

Carl figured that the people he killed were no great loss to society. Hell, they were already crooks or so deeply involved with crooks to the point they were on a hit list. Chances were they were not nice people themselves. He got to know enough about them while preparing to terminate them to confirm that to his satisfaction.

He had decided years ago that he would refuse to kill someone he didn't think deserved to be shot. He had turned down one contract for that reason.

The weekly poker group was his reality check. He liked to observe the interplay between these men. He and his wife socialized with individual members of the group. He occasionally played golf with two or three of the guys. Everything was light and casual.

Hit by the Dealer

Carl wasn't a Wise Guy; he had no interest in that life style or those people.

The deal progressed around the table. Tom to Carl's left was the present dealer and passed out two cards to each of them. That made Carl the "small blind".

Like most people now, they played Texas Hold'em. It's an apparently simple game which people think is mostly luck. That's what makes it popular. People don't realize that it's not just a game of chance.

What Carl enjoyed most about the game was the psychological aspect. As described in the Kenny Rogers song, reading people's faces, guessing what their cards were, understanding the odds, and deciding when to raise, check, or fold, is the nature of the game. Anyone can win with good cards. It's winning as much as possible with good cards and occasionally winning with bad cards that makes the game interesting.

Contract killing is a little like that. You want a clean kill with as little fuss as possible. And if the odds look bad you want to pass and wait for another hand.

Also, like poker, the longer you are involved in tracking someone the higher the stakes get. In poker the blinds and the ante keep creeping higher. The longer you stay in a hand, the greater amount you have committed to the pot and the greater the pressure to stay in as the bets rise. The longer you tail someone, the higher the chance of getting picked up and picked off.

In his working life, which he thought of to himself as problem solving, he tried to keep his engagement time to a minimum but to learn as much as he could. The longer you are in an area and the closer you come to the target, the more chance you will be spotted or leave a clue which can be traced afterwards.

It is a fine balance between learning enough and hanging around too long. It was always best to observe from a point of safety, identify the best time and place early, and then once you are committed, do it quickly and get out.

Some decisions are easy to make. For example, in this poker hand the three and six off suit which had been dealt as his down cards made it easy to decide not to call. His most recent contract had been almost as easy a decision.

Chapter 4

A new deal

A new set of cards dealt out provides an opportunity to act.

Carl had found a signal message in the inbox of a private e-mail box he checked frequently. That message led him to call Stan on a safe line. That in turn led to a package being sent to a mail drop in Houston in the name he was born with, Wolf Hiltz.

That would be forwarded by mail to Buffalo in another package with just a Postal Box number where Carl picked it up. Yes, it was complicated and it cost something to maintain, but Carl regarded it as a life line. Usually one held on to a life line to be saved. This life line worked the other way; safety would come by letting go.

All he need do was to close, or just stop paying for the postal box in Buffalo and all contact with him would disappear. Carl never went near Houston; he just sent them a payment each year and occasionally contacted them by phone if there was some additional service he required, such as changing the forwarding address. He often speculated that if he did quit he might take one last precaution of changing the forwarding address to South America.

This time Stan forwarded an assignment which would involve a visit to Miami. That part was good. In Miami a huge percentage of the people are tourists, and most of them are there for a short time. There are lots of conventions. A new arrival would not even be noticed.

These days it was hard to take a gun on an airline unless you had a competition permit and a special travel case. Carl had both, but preferred not to use them. It was best not to attract attention by doing that. Of course, Carl had built up a supply of safe guns around the country so it was also possible to fly somewhere nearby, such as Atlanta where he had a stash. Atlanta was a hub. It was easy to connect through there.

There is a traveler's joke about a saint and a sinner meeting up in Atlanta on the way to heaven and hell respectively. You have to pass through Atlanta to go anywhere was the point.

Whenever it was practicable, Carl preferred to drive to the destination. There was less of a paper trail, since he paid cash for everything when on a job. Also, it meant he was free from airline schedules and could make an instant adjustment to his plans.

Home for Carl was Niagara Falls, Canada. He could catch a flight from Buffalo (which was just across the border) to Atlanta. Miami was an easy drive from Atlanta. He could rent a car in Atlanta, drive into Florida and then rent another car there. That way he would have local plates and the car he used in Miami would be history a few hours after "John" was history also.

The tricky part was the target himself. This target, Carl always referred to them all as "John," was already aware that a lot of people would like him dead. He usually had bodyguards and was armed and careful.

As soon as Carl had a few pertinent facts about "John," he had his reservations about the contract. The information he already knew about the target was working its way through his mind as he flew south to Atlanta.

He had almost been killed many years ago when someone unexpectedly showed up in the middle of a hit and he had no back-up gun. If this target was as protected as he seemed, one back-up gun would not be enough.

Chapter 5

The "Nuts"

A term meaning the best possible hand that can be made with the five cards turned up and two down cards; an unbeatable hand.

He arrived in Atlanta Sunday evening, rented a car and checked into a hotel near the airport. For business he traveled with a tool kit of simple tools of the trade. One set of tools was kept in a safety deposit box in Atlanta. Monday morning, he picked it up on the way through Atlanta and tucked it under the back seat.

Carl liked playing it safe. He always rented a full sized car because of the extra protection in the event of a crash and he drove defensively. Getting shot was an acceptable occupational risk; the idea of being killed in an automobile accident seemed absurd.

When he arrived in West Palm Beach he checked into a motel for the night and examined, cleaned, oiled, and loaded the tools in his tool kit.

In the kit he carried a Smith & Wesson seven-shot revolver in .22 caliber and a back up snub nosed, hammerless S & W .38 special. Carl owned several of each model.

Revolvers had been chosen for several reasons. Semi-automatic pistols can jam, occasionally do. Rounds can misfire, in which case a semi has to be racked by hand to fire. With a revolver you just pull the trigger again. The major problem with semi-automatic pistols is that they spew spent casings in all directions. Revolvers keep them neatly contained. Carl didn't plan to spend time searching under cars or bodies for little pieces of brass.

There are net or cage-like devices designed to catch the ejected brass. The problem with those is threefold. First they occasionally bounced the brass back into the mechanism, thereby increasing the chance of a stovepipe style jam. Second they made the weapon less streamlined and more likely to get caught on something, or someone. Third they look stupid. Carl would be embarrassed to be caught with one.

Carl loaded his own ammunition. This saved him from making frequent trips to gun shops. Not that that alone would attract much attention in America. By loading his own rounds he could load light on the powder which kept the noise down and avoided over or under penetration.

He had purchased a Dillon progressive reloader system which allowed him to load the type of slug and the size of charge he preferred for .38 caliber. Normally he used a .22 with a light, or "target" load. Those he could purchase with no problem at all because most people used them at club matches. And .22 caliber is a real pain to self load because they are almost always rim fire cartridges. You can't just stick a primer in the centre of the brass.

Once he had needed to use special .38 slugs to penetrate body armor. The slugs, which are copper plated and coated with a slippery plastic, were available from a small Toronto company. If you load your own rounds you can load hot enough to turn a .38 special into what are commonly called "cop killers" because they will penetrate body armor. But, ready-made cartridges of that capacity are not available in an over-the-counter purchase.

In fact, Carl had never shot a police officer. He didn't believe he had ever shot anyone who wasn't a criminal or worse.

He had once overheard a couple guys discussing the merits of a .357 over a .38. What a joke that was. Most people don't realize that a .357 and a .38 slug are exactly the same diameter, .357 mm.

It came about because when the first .38 caliber revolvers were made they tended to blow up. That was because the black powder used at the time went off with too sharp an initial shock. To correct the problem, rather than create a whole new mould for the revolver itself, the manufacturers just reduced the size of the barrel which was drilled into it from .380 to .357. They didn't change the name and so today we find both .357 and .38 being produced but firing similar bullets. The brass casing on a standard .38 is shorter to fit into a short cylinder; a person getting hit by a .38 special or .357 would not notice the difference.

Usually Carl preferred to use the .22 because he almost always worked at close range and it made less fuss. If you fired once, or even twice, most people hearing it would not even think of a gun shot. Also, a .22 fired into a skull will bounce back and forth, mashing the brain up nicely without coming out the other side.

His .38 was carried only in case he encountered opposition. It wouldn't always knock someone down, like a Colt 1911 .45 ACP, but if the shot was accurate it would kill. Carl was accurate.

He belonged to a local gun club, Pine Hill, in St Catharines where he shot in bull's eye competitions, as target shooting is usually called, and where he went quiet afternoons for serious practice. He even had a permit which allowed him to carry a gun across the border for matches in Tonawanda and other clubs. It was almost impossible to get a carry permit in Canada, but collectors and competitors could transport guns to and from matches. Whenever possible he didn't use the registered guns for business. For that, he had an ample supply in the States, "across the river" as locals referred to the American side. Occasionally he had used the two he kept at the gun club in Tonawanda.

He liked the .38 because it was compact and being hammerless wouldn't snag on something if you needed to draw it quickly. If you needed it, chances were you needed it quickly. He wore it in an ankle holster on his left foot. That way he could draw it while still holding his main weapon. Being able to shoot with either hand was a required skill.

He shot at the police range from time to time in friendly competition. One of the competition styles, Police Pistol Competition, stressed the need to be able to shoot with either hand, and although most officers carried a semi automatic pistol while on duty, the competitions favored use of a revolver and speed loaders, (devices which could be carried attached to one's belt and would insert six cartages at once into a revolver).

After breakfast at the motel he drove into the long term parking area at West Palm Beach airport at 10:00 Monday morning. He parked in a spot with a few empty places nearby and walked into the arrivals area carrying the nondescript suitcase which now also contained his tool kit.

His rental car was waiting for him under the name Calvin Bridges. The driver's license had been obtained with some difficulty and the credit card was in good standing. He had created a credit rating for Cal Bridges many years ago and made regular purchases and payments to keep it active and in good standing.

It is almost impossible to do some things without a credit card. Renting a car is one of them. Also, if he did need to fly on business he didn't want to do it under his own name. Unfortunately, new regulations would prevent him presenting it when crossing the U.S.-Canada border.

It was reassuring to know that there would be no record of Carl Hill being anywhere near the site of a crime. Small details often prove to be important and trip people up. Carl remembered the ridiculous mistake the bombers of the World Trade Center had made in 1993 by going back to get their deposit on their rental van. If they had just kept running they might have got away.

The good news for society is that most criminals are not too bright. There are often articles in the news describing how a gang of six or seven would-be bank robbers plan a job for two months, steal a get-away vehicle and then divide a total of twenty or thirty thousand dollars. That's only about six thousand each. Hell, you could make that much in two months doing a simple job with no danger of going to jail.

Carl wanted more money and less risk of being caught.

His rental cars never attracted that kind of attention, but he also tried to avoid getting fines or tickets while driving them. Son of Sam had been caught almost by accident because of a parking ticket. If Carl did get a ticket near a contract hit location, that fine would be paid off promptly using Cal Bridges' identity.

Chapter 6

Gut-Shot Straight Draw

Some hands have less chance of filling than others. There is an adage that one should never draw to an inside straight. The ugliest inside straight to draw to is one in which it is the middle card of five missing. This draw is called a "Gut-Shot Straight Draw" probably because drawing to it usually results in a lot of pain.

The early September sky was blue, the traffic moderate, the car an unexceptional four door sedan. As he drove south toward Miami he maintained a steady two or three miles per hour over the limit. No trooper would stop him at that speed.

He knew where he could probably get a good look at "John" in a public place, a restaurant he was reported to favor for lunch. Carl always liked to get a personal view of a target. Photos and data told one story, but personal impressions were important to Carl.

He had reserved a room at a hotel that was mid-range and near "John's" place of business on the edge of midtown. It had its own parking lot attached to the main building and a small restaurant.

He checked in and bought a map of the city at a small shop. He located "John's" home in upscale northeastern section of Miami. The house was on a cul de sac. This made an approach there a major obstacle, but Carl hadn't expected to be able to do anything at "John's" home. "John" was probably a piece of shit, but his wife and kids might be okay. Carl didn't want to cause collateral damage.

Just to get a sense of the location, Carl drove through the neighborhood. Large houses sat on large lots with the likelihood that a strange car would be noticed. He didn't even turn down the dead end "John" lived on. Interesting term Dead End, he thought. There could be some irony there.

He drove back to the hotel and parked the car. He would call home, watch a ball game or a movie in his room with a room service meal and get a good night's sleep. Tomorrow was another working day.

Chapter 7

Call or Fold

The decision to match the bet or to drop out.

Waking up with a definite goal in mind was always a bit special.

Carl was focused and prepared. But he was neither eager nor nervous.

He had coffee at the hotel while reading the local paper. He read with interest about some of the bonuses being paid to bankers and CEO's for running companies that lost money. Conrad Black was even out on bail. Now that was criminal.

At 11:45, wearing a business suit and looking as common as the next man, he walked one block to the area near "John's" office, and went into the restaurant where he knew he usually took lunch. He bought another newspaper and settled into a booth away from the window but near the front door and facing back toward the rear of the restaurant.

If "John" didn't come there today for lunch, Carl would have to find a location from which he could see him when he left the office for the day. By preference he would like to see him over lunch interacting with someone. It would also allow Carl to observe "John's" bodyguards in action to evaluate how serious the protection was.

About ten minutes later two guys came in and checked out everyone, including Carl. They were not discrete about it either. They looked him over and talked while looking at him and a couple other people before they made a phone call. One of the two guards then went over and sat in a booth at the back. The other went through a door to check out the kitchen and then stood along the wall beside that door.

When "John" arrived it was like the arrival of the Pope. He was with two other men who were so obviously carrying that they might as well have had the guns in their hands. There was another man with "John" who seemed to be a business associate. "John" went to the booth where one of his henchmen was sitting. When he got there, that guard got up and went out to the sidewalk in front of the restaurant.

That table had clearly been picked out in advance for the security of the location. One of the men who had come in with "John" sat down with his back to the wall. "John" sat down beside him and his "associate" sat down across from him. The second guard walked to a table at the other corner from "John" and sat down where he could watch the main door of the restaurant.

"John" and his guest ordered a meal, but none of his working men ate. The restaurant staff seemed used to this. The security people were left to do as they liked.

Carl ordered a salad. While he ate and read he watched while twenty minutes of the scenario played out. Whenever anyone came into the restaurant, came out of the kitchen, or got up from one of the tables, at least three sets of eyes were on him or her.

Twenty minutes of watching was enough for Carl. He asked for his bill, paid it, and walked out. He went to a public phone and called Stan. His call was short and to the point. "I had a nice visit, but I'm leaving here now. It's not really my kind of place. I'll be in touch."

Carl went into a bookstore he noticed earlier and picked up some light reading, one of John Sanford's *Prey* series. He walked back to his hotel, and settled in for a quiet evening.

In the morning he drove back to West Palm Beach and turned in his rental car. He had no second thoughts about his decision. Stan would be able to find some young guy wanting to prove how good he was. Carl would rather sit this one out.

He had spent a bit of money on the flight, the two rental cars, and the motel and hotel. But that was just money. Being dead was serious.

Although he felt secure in his decision to turn down this job, he knew it would cause Stan to wonder about his reliability. Carl always reserved the right to turn down a hit. But if his turn down rate ever got too high, Stan might stop referring contracts to him. Carl suspected anything above 5% might be too high.

In twenty-five years he had turned down three contracts out of eighty. So, this one brought him up against his self-imposed guideline. Well, he thought, if it's over, it's over. He had been careful for a quarter of a century. He wasn't going to throw it all away for one last job.

In poker the last hand may strip you of everything. Better to sit out the last hand, even to give up playing the game, than lose it all. He had enough chips already. He didn't need to continue to play.

Would he be content to spend the rest of his life without the thrill of what he'd earned his living at? Damn right he would. If he needed a thrill he could always take up skydiving.

Chapter 8

Bully

A player with a big stack of chips may bet big to intimidate others.

After an hour of play, the poker table had been reduced to three players: Carl, Tom, and Dave. Tom had about twice as big a stack of chips as either of the others.

Carl knew that at this point Dave would play it safe. Dave would focus on not being the next one knocked out. Second place paid a consolation prize. He'd rather be second than take a chance on being first at the risk of being eliminated. Dave was an accountant by profession and by lifestyle. He was not a risk taker. He wore conservative clothes, he drove a mid-sized sedan, and he had bought his house based on the fact that he knew that houses of that style were easy to resell and held their value.

This was a crucial turning point in the game. Carl decided that he would face off against Tom with a reasonable hand but avoid a head to head against Dave unless he had "the nuts," meaning the best hand possible with the cards showing.

Tom was a good player, but with a big stack he was prone to try to "buy" a pot by raising a lot to drive other players out. If a player folds, he can't win. Sometimes that approach works. If you let another player intimidate you, he will grind down your stack to the point that you can't make a meaningful bet.

The other three had drifted over to the other side of the games room and were discussing the pennant race. There was some interest in the possibility of Texas being in it, though the Giants had their support here too.

Baseball was one game that Carl had enjoyed as a spectator specifically because you didn't have to pay attention about 90% of the time. The pitcher threw a ball, nothing happened, then a bit later he threw another one. When someone hit the ball the action was fast and furious, then everything reverted to the same slow pace.

You could have a decent conversation at a baseball game. Try doing that at football or hockey. There you were expected to watch every move or risk missing something important.

Tom was now trying to bully the other players with his bigger stack, so when Carl caught a pair of tens down and the ten of diamonds came up on the flop along with a Queen of spades and a four of hearts, he perked up.

He checked and let Tom make a pushy bet. Dave folded and Carl took his time deciding and then called with apparent reluctance.

A second four, this time a club, came up on the turn and Carl checked again. Tom made a bet that doubled the pot and would require Carl to put in about a quarter of his remaining stack to stay.

Carl looked at his cards again while hoping that Tom had a third four down to keep him betting. Then he called again with feigned hesitation.

When an off suit Jack of clubs came up on the river, Carl was sitting with a full-house, tens over fours with only three hands which could beat him. If Tom had two fours down, two jacks down, or two queens down, Tom would win; anything else and the hand belonged to Carl.

Carl could check again hoping Tom would have a good but lesser hand and would bet or that Tom would not have a good hand but would try to "buy the pot." On the other hand, Carl could make a small bet and hope that Tom would raise. On yet another hypothetical hand, Carl could go all in and hope Tom would think that Carl was bluffing.

Carl hoped that Tom had bought his apparently reluctant betting so far and would try to drive him out. He checked once more.

"All in," Tom declared, thereby putting pressure on Carl. Fold or be knocked out, his tone seemed to say.

These were the moments which made Texas Hold'em so interesting, Carl thought.

"Okay, I'm all in too," he said with a shrug.

"Straight to the Ace," Tom crowed, showing an Ace and King of hearts.

"Nice draw," Carl responded, turning his winning full-house face up. He waited quietly while Dave assisted Tom in matching up piles of chips and pushing them over to Carl.

The effect of winning that pot was that it neatly reversed Carl's position with Tom. Carl, with about half of the total, could settle into a careful game in which he let Tom take risks when Dave was in while he only played if the odds seemed on his side.

True to form, after a few hands Tom pushed against Dave when Dave had good cards and Tom was almost cleaned out when Dave won the hand.

Then in desperation Tom went all in on the next hand and Dave collected the last of his chips with two nines.

This part of the game was totally different from the game up until the two-person face-off. Now any hand could win and it was closer to being a true game of luck than the preceding sparing had been.

After a few folds and all-ins by each of them, Dave had a nice run of hands in which Carl had too much to fold and not enough to win. Dave had just over half of the chips when Carl peeked at his cards and discovered a pair of Kings. He went all-in and Dave called.

When they turned up their hands, Dave showed an Ace and Jack of spades. The flop yielded two more spades, six and ten and a Jack of hearts. The four of clubs added nothing on the turn, but the river was an Ace of diamonds which gave Dave two pair, as well as top pair, to defeat Carl.

Could have gone either way, they both agreed and moved over to join the others for a final beer.

"Anyone for golf on Saturday?" Terry asked. "Weather report looks good."

Carl and Joyce had plans for a special dinner at home Saturday, so Carl deferred, but Darren said he was up for it.

Tom and Russ said they'd check their schedules and give Terry a call.

A few minutes later they called it a night and drifted out to their respective cars.

Carl drove home thinking that perhaps he should consider making that farewell call to Stan. Better to take control and quit while he was on top. He didn't want to hang on becoming more and more cautious until Stan stopped asking him to take on a job. No one likes rejection.

Cold blooded killers have feelings too, he thought, and laughed at his own joke.

Life was good and one never knew when that pesky Ace might turn up to ruin a good thing.

Chapter 9

Money Management

As in life, a player must build up and dispense cash or chips with care.

When he woke up the sun was shining in the window and Joyce was pulling back the inner curtains to look out over the back garden. Joyce had turned 46 this past June just two weeks after he had. For some reason, genetic he supposed, she still had not a single grey hair. Her brown eyes suited her auburn hair; he found himself wondering how they would look when her hair turned grey. He pictured that and decided she would be just as beautiful to him.

She noticed that he was awake and said "Looks like a glorious day. Do you have anything that needs doing?"

"Nothing pressing," he responded. "Is there something you want to do?"

"Well... I was wondering if you could give me some advice about a listing I've been offered." Joyce surprised him by saying.

Joyce and he hardly ever talked business. He never talked about his and she seldom mentioned hers except when she made a sale and they celebrated with a glass of bubbly or by going out to dinner somewhere special.

Carl was proud of how competent Joyce was at her job. She took great trouble to research the market and to write ads which were a cut above the normal agent ads which were full of clichés. He understood from meeting some of her fellow agents that she was well liked and thought to have a successful and promising future.

Certainly she was doing well financially. He had assisted her in setting up a ladder of bond investments such that a new set of ten-year bonds would renew every year to maximize profit and keep ten percent available any given year. The first renewal would be in a couple years from now, he remembered. Joyce had been showing a reasonable profit at real estate sales for about nine years now. That alone would indicate that she was doing well.

"I know nothing about real estate," he said. "How can I give you advice?"

"Well, normally I wouldn't ask you, but this is a business listing. The present owner says it could be a real money maker. I can't be sure if he's exaggerating or not. I also thought that you could give me a few ideas about how I could promote it to a prospective buyer."

"Okay, why not?" he said. "Where is it?"

"That's the other thing. It's not in an area which I would normally think of as commercial. It's on a side road out near the Welland Airport."

"What kind of business opportunity does it offer, according to the seller? And why doesn't he develop it himself?" Carl asked, his voice showing a hint of skepticism

"I've got a file I prepared which has details he provided. If you'd like to look it over that will give you a better picture," Joyce said. From the small reading table she used by the window she picked up a manila file folder bulging with documents and placed it on the edge of the dresser near him.

Carl carried the file downstairs and set it on a chair beside his office door. He wanted to look over his investments today anyway. He'd like to be certain about his finances if he was really going to retire from his present income producing activities.

He would like to calculate just how much he could generate to sustain a life with no other source of income. Eventually Social Security, if it still existed, would kick in, but Carl had just turned 46 and he would like to base his income planning to include a long healthy retirement.

He picked up the morning paper from outside the front door and came into the kitchen where Joyce was pouring coffee. "I'll take a look at that folder today," he told her. "Are you going into the office?"

"Yes, I'm on duty this morning. We could meet for lunch if you like."

"Sure, I'll meet you at Sammy's. When will you be free?"

"How about 1:00? I've got this afternoon open."

"Fine," he said and fished the business section out of the paper before passing the rest over to Joyce.

While Joyce gathered a few things together Carl picked up the manila folder and headed into his office. Most of the documents he found were legal documents referring to the offer of sale and the agent permission sheets. He looked at the description sheet, which resembled ones he'd seen in Joyce's MLS books. The property was described as rural/commercial with 165 acres of land bordered by two roads.

There was a picture of a brick farm house and two steel clad out buildings. The asking price, $1,400,000 seemed a bit high to him, but he was no expert on rural property prices.

Six sheets were attached to this description page which contained a spreadsheet presentation and a business plan. The proposed name for the business surprised him: Sunshine Nature Spa.

"I'll see you at 1:00," Joyce called as she headed out into the attached garage.

"Right, at Sammy's," he replied.

Now what would make the owner of this property think it would work as a nature spa, he wondered. As he read through the documentation, the proposal started to make sense.

The aspects which made this plot of land of possible interest were laid out in the plan. It had an old quarry, now filled with spring water and it had a gas well.

Many of the farms in the area had tapped into the natural gas which was trapped beneath the area. Some of them used it for drying corn or soya bean crops. A few even used it for heating the buildings of dairy operations. Under federal regulation, each farm has unlimited use of the gas from a well, or wells, on the property, but the gas could not be sold for use off the property.

The business proposed in the plan was that the gas be used to heat the clear water of the lake formed by the old quarry and that a spa, recreation centre, retreat, gourmet restaurant, wine tasting centre, and hotel be built. For winter use, some cross country ski trails could be developed and the wooded sections could be nature walks.

Some rough sketches accompanied the plan which showed the extent of the property, the wooded areas, the location and size of the quarry, and a proposal for where a small hotel and recreation centre could be situated.

The idea intrigued Carl. Would there be demand for such a venture? Rather, he thought, could demand be generated with clever advertising?

He set the folder aside and began an examination of his financial resources. Their house was mortgage free and probably worth more than the $700,000 they had paid for it. Both he and Joyce had almost new cars. His was a Mercedes 300E, chosen largely because it is one of the safest cars in the world in a collision. Joyce had an AWD Audi which served her well in all weather conditions.

With his dividend paying stocks and bonds and his "company purchased" annuity, Carl could draw almost as much as he was already declaring per year without reducing the principal.

That didn't even include the cash in his offshore corporate accounts or the property his corporation owned outright in Spain and Bermuda. The property in Spain was rented long term and brought in more than its annual carrying costs. The Bermuda office was a corporate write-off. But it also had an efficiency apartment which he sometimes rented from himself.

The files concerning the corporations were on a laptop that was never connected on-line or to other computers. The best firewall is a stand-alone computer. No one can hack into a computer they never have contact with.

When he considered the total of his holdings he decided that, although he would never be mentioned in Forbes magazine, he had enough.

Yes, it was time to quit killing people. There would always be jerks and assholes deserving to be shot; other shooters would just have to pick up the slack.

Carl closed down his spreadsheet and moved into the living room. Their home along the Niagara Parkway backed onto the river. From their window, they had a view across the Niagara Gorge to the American side.

This house was one of very few on the river side of the road. It was because of Joyce's professional connections that they had learned when it went up for sale five years ago. It was private while being well located between Niagara Falls and Niagara-on-the-Lake. The properties here were expensive and in demand.

He sat for a moment looking out the window contemplating the future.

One of his favorite comic strips was Calvin and Hobbes. He remembered one episode in which Calvin was building a substandard snowman and explaining to Hobbes that "Success consists of setting your goal low enough that you've already achieved it."

Carl decided that although he had set a significant financial goal, he had succeeded.

Chapter 10

Play your cards close to the vest

To avoid others seeing your cards, you keep them close to you.

Leaves were starting to show fall colours. Carl pulled out of the driveway onto the Niagara Parkway. Running, as it does, along the Niagara River and joining Niagara-on-the-Lake with Niagara Falls, the parkway had long been one of his favourite drives. Even before Joyce and he had bought their present house, they had often gone out of their way to take it. It continued past Niagara Falls itself and ultimately ended in Fort Erie, the Canadian town across the river from Buffalo.

There were very few cars as he drove slowly toward Queenston. The tourists who frequented Niagara-on-the-Lake and Niagara Falls during the summer months had returned to their homes leaving both tourist centres relatively quiet.

While passing the war memorial in Queenston he glanced up at the familiar tower on the heights commemorating General Isaac Brock's repulsion of American troops in the war of 1812. Soldiers were remembered by monuments; he expected, hoped, not to be remembered. On the other hand, he had been better paid for his occasional use of a gun than common soldiers were.

He also hadn't had to wear a uniform or march up and down while drill sergeants bawled commands.

He continued south past the Queenston bridge and the hydro power stations and on toward downtown Niagara Falls. Golfers were out on the golf course which ran beside the roadway. Since this was Wednesday he imagined they must be doctors and dentists.

Perhaps not, he thought. Despite the jokes to that effect, he had always believed that most doctors were dedicated individuals who worked hard as well and deserved their income.

Carl often held silent conversations with himself. It made it easier to avoid expressing opinions to others. He wondered, not for the first time, if other people talked to themselves as he did.

Right now for example, he was having a quiet debate about the salaries of rock stars and professional athletes and the money they earned. Were pro golfers athletes or entertainers, he asked himself. As far as that went, were politicians comedians or crooks?

Now, now, he chided himself. Some people might think that it was wrong for him to be paid to kill people. He had to chuckle a bit as he contemplated what most people would say if he started telling them he was a retired hit man.

'What business were you in,' he imagined someone asking at a cocktail party.

'I used to put bullets into heads,' he would reply and watch their expression.

Well maybe not, he told himself.

Now the tower of the casino came into sight. Carl did not enjoy the Disneyland characteristic of the casino; nor did he want to play where the house had an advantage.

What little gambling he did was restricted to his Tuesday night poker and the occasional lottery ticket for some charity. Even if he didn't win, he didn't mind contributing his money to either cause.

Joyce and he had visited the new Niagara casino a few times with other couples, but just for a bit of entertainment. They had even gone to Las Vegas once on a four-night holiday. But even there they had mostly enjoyed some shows, a few good meals and walked the strip to observe the spectacles of the volcano at The Mirage and the Belaggio fountains.

Carl didn't believe there was any risk of meeting people he had known in New York at the tables, or have them recognize him from surveillance cameras. But, as one of the gangland dons in the movie Casino remarked, "Why take chances?"

Now at the end of his career he thought back to his beginnings. It seemed a long time ago. It seemed almost a different life.

Chapter 11

Learning the game

Rules, card handling, even how to bet, are things that have to be learned.

As a young teenager growing up in New York in the late 70's, Carl, well, Wolf then, had always been on the fringes of crime. He had stolen a few cars, robbed a few small stores, and helped out in a few burglaries. But mostly he had played it smart even then.

He usually chose a role with less risk. He would be the look out, or he would drive the get away car. In fact the get away just involved driving back to someone's place to split up the take. His was normally a smaller portion, but then he took fewer chances too.

Many of the people he ran with were arrested; they seemed almost to enjoy the prestige that gave them. Wolf had never been caught. Local police knew he was one of the local hoods, but his name never made its way onto a court docket. Partially that was good luck; partially it was good judgment.

Whatever it was, it meant that in his early twenties he had no criminal record and yet had connections with some professional criminals. Once he was involved in a bad situation and he had to shoot someone. He hadn't enjoyed doing it; but he had done it. He had been a "standup guy" and it had been noticed.

That was when one of the people he knew, a person with serious connections, invited him to meet Stan. Stan was a sort of matchmaker. He made connections between people who wanted something done without anyone knowing who had ordered it and people who, for a fee, would do it without knowing why.

It was an unusual niche which Stan occupied. He had created it. There may have been other people who ran agencies similar to Stan's, but Wolf had never heard or read about such a thing. The offer interested him.

He knew that there was good money to be made as a hit man. After all, it was a dangerous activity paid for by people for whom money was readily available. The question he asked himself was could he do it with some degree of safety?

It wasn't as if Wolf had a lot of job offers. School had just been a place he went until he was 17. It was there he learned to smoke, and fight, and get along. He was 15 when he stole his first car and 16 when he assisted in boosting some electronic equipment from a warehouse. There hadn't been many role models who would have encouraged him to consider Wall Street, or banking, or even learning a trade. He'd enjoyed woodworking and machine shop, but he didn't think he'd enjoy a life at a 9 to 5 job.

His father had been a drunk and a truck driver, but he drank better than he drove, so he died when he drove off the road one night. Wolf hadn't seen him much and didn't miss him much.

He hadn't hated his father, he just hadn't liked him. Wolf's mom had worked on the cleaning staff of a small hotel which specialized in rooms rented by the hour. When Wolf was 18, his mother was killed in the crossfire of a shoot-out between cops and a pimp.

Some would think that that would put Wolf off guns. On the contrary, it made him want to have a gun so he could shoot back.

It had been said, mostly by the NRA, that "Only a slave can't have a gun." Wolf believed that if others all have guns you had better have one too. The only people Wolf knew who had money were crooks and they all had guns. Wolf knew he would like to have money.

Wolf was smart enough to realize that the average small time hood either remained that or was killed or sent to jail. Being a big time hood didn't seem likely either with his lack of family connections and his ancestry which was a mixture of British, French and German. Maybe the offer Stan was making him was his best chance out of the 'hood.

He also understood that killing a person important enough that a hit man was hired, there was a good chance that he would leave family or business partners behind who would want to take revenge.

The only way to avoid being the subject of that revenge was to be untouchable. A "Made Man" was untouchable, but Wolf hadn't even been to Italy and although he enjoyed pizza that wasn't going to help much. So, the only way for Wolf to be untouchable was to be out of touch. In other words, he would have to make sure that no one knew that he had made the hit and no one could find him. Could he do that? Wolf thought he might just be able to.

That was his start. At first Stan knew all about Wolf, but after the first job that changed.

His first target was a minor thug in a New York City borough. Stan was offering him $10,000 to do the hit. It was all to be paid up front too. Stan wasn't worried about trusting Wolf to do what he was being paid to do. Wolf knew better than to cheat people who hired hit men.

That wasn't a lot of money in 1985. Wolf knew that it was peanuts compared to what an out-of-town hit man would get. He also knew that it was a test. If he screwed up it was a one off; if he did well there might be more to come.

Stan was in it for the long run. He had a stable of talent and he was looking for more.

Wolf thought about the target of the hit he was assigned to. This guy was nothing special. Anyone could find him and kill him. What was interesting was that someone was willing to pay so that no one could trace it back to him. That meant that there was someone big involved somehow.

Wolf realized that this was his big chance. He would do the hit, and he would make sure that he wouldn't be hit back.

The hit itself was easy. The target was just waiting to be wasted. It was an easy task to follow him and shoot him as he walked to his car late one night.

The significant part was what Wolf did next. He didn't just go to see Stan and say "Hey, I did good." Instead, he left town.

Wolf had a car. It wasn't a great car, but it ran well. He drove out of the city that night with everything he needed to start a new life in the car with him. He drove north up the Hudson River then west.

He stayed that night in a motel and the next day arrived in Elmira, NY. Wolf figured that no one he knew had even heard of Elmira. Wolf had picked it off the map as being basically nowhere. At the same time, it was near Highway 86 if he wanted to go somewhere.

Then he set about becoming Carl.

Chapter 12

A Fish

The term suggests that a player is not very good, a sucker, a mark, a loser waiting to be gobbled up.

As he drove into Niagara Falls, Carl stayed along the river until he came to Clifton Hill, the heart of the tacky tourist area. He turned right and drove away from the river. At Victoria Ave. he turned left and drove past the shops offering souvenirs made in China and the restaurants offering all day breakfasts and all-you-can-eat salad bars.

When he reached the string of hotels and motels which offered 'easy access to the casino' and 'minutes to the Falls,' he started thinking about the proposal in the manila file Joyce had given him.

Part of Carl really did think like an entrepreneur. The idea of a retreat of the type described did make sense. But it would require some specialized knowledge and a fairly large monetary investment.

He pulled into Sammy's just before 1:00 and noticed Joyce's car already there.

Sammy's was an institution in the area. It had been there been since 1946. That was probably longer than any of the present staff had been alive. He didn't know much about the original Sammy. The restaurant served good food and the cheerful energy of the staff suggested that the present owners were easy to work for. Carl picked up moods and ambient tension in situations. It was a survival skill which also came in handy playing poker.

Joyce was in a booth in the older part of the restaurant. He slid in across from her and placed the manila file on the table beside the old juke box each booth still had.

"I'm thinking of the fish and chips," Joyce informed him.

"On Wednesday?" he quipped.

"Anything to help out the Portuguese fisher folk," she responded.

Carl had once told her that legend had it that the Catholic Church had decreed fish for Fridays in order to provide a monetary boost to the fishing industry. It had become a running joke between them.

"Good enough. I think I'll have a small though. I feel a bit too large already." In fact Carl never seemed to gain or lose weight. It was something Joyce had noticed and mentioned to him with a hint of envy in her voice. Joyce was fetchingly slim, but it was because she worked at it.

Deciding what to have was not difficult at Sammy's. They only served fish and chips, fish without chips, chips without fish, and hamburgers. At least 19 out of 20 customers ordered the fish and chips.

The only decision was usually whether to order one or two pieces of fish. The orders were placed at a counter and relayed verbally into the kitchen by the counter staff. Customers were so used to hearing the order transmitted as "small" or "large" that all the regular customers usually said just "small" or "large" themselves when ordering.

After placing an order, the customer paid and was issued a slip of paper with a number. A notice posted behind the counter stated: "Numbers may not be called out in order." Carl had once tried to joke by asking the counterperson if that was a rule or a warning. The young girl just looked confused so he didn't bother explaining.

Sammy's had been a strong supporter of local athletics over the past 50 some years. There were photos of hockey and softball teams in uniforms bearing the Sammy's logo and one for the Burlington Chiefs lacrosse team. Carl had heard that the owners also supported young players by preferentially employing them at the restaurant. Prominent among the press clippings and photos on the wall was a photo of the then young Wayne Gretsky seated beside Gordie Howe. Howe had his hockey stick hooked playfully around Wayne's neck.

One of Carl's favorite photos was one of the Sudbury Cub Wolves, Nickel Belt Champions of 1934. It was one of the teams shown which was not local. Carl wondered what the story was behind that. There was also a newspaper clipping with a picture of Sammy dressed up in full fisherman's regalia and leaning against the service counter at his restaurant. He looked like a bit of a character.

Carl went back to the booth to wait for his number to be called.

Joyce had the file over in front of her and an expectant look on her face.

"I looked it over. I think the proposal and sketch business plan make a lot of sense," he told her. "I might even be interested myself."

"Are you kidding? Would you want to run a resort?"

"Absolutely not," he assured her. "I meant as an investment for one of the companies I consult for. They have some property holdings and own some hotels. If they were involved it would be as a silent partner."

"Do you think it could make money?"

"Probably, if it were run properly. I'd like to look at the property in person, of course. But, a retreat, spa, health club would certainly have appeal. Being close to the Falls, the Casino, the Shaw Festival and the Fort Erie race track wouldn't hurt either."

"It's a bit close to the airport. Do you think that would be a problem?"

"There can't be more than ten or twenty small planes in and out of there per day in good weather. Besides, that could be a selling point for overpaid executives with access to a corporate plane," he assured her. "As long as it is upscale enough."

"Would you like to go and look at it today?" Joyce asked. "If you like it we can get some earthmovers in there tomorrow morning to start construction," she said with a straight face.

"I can see why you're doing well," Carl responded. "But, yes. If you're free let's have a look at it."

At that point their number was called by the counter staff. "We'd better eat up," Carl joked. "We don't want to be evicted."

It was an old point of amusement to them in reference to a sign posted in the booths: 'To Avoid Excessive Loitering We Have A 30 Min. Time Limit.'

Chapter 13

A handle

A nickname by which a player may be known.

Wolf had chosen to be known as Wolf because it was better than the alternatives. His first name was actually Wolfgang and his second name Amadeus. His full name at birth was Wolfgang Amadeus Hiltz. Those two names may have worked for Mozart, but this was not a good choice for a young boy born in post WWII America. Nonetheless, it was his name.

He had done the best he could as a child by insisting on the shorter and less German sounding name Wolf. Anyone named Amadeus or Wolfgang would have lasted about 10 minutes in the 'hood.

Now he had another chance in a new place. Wolf's first action was to find a place to live in Elmira. It had to be cheap so he chose a boarding house just north of Church Street. His next action to start a new identity was to introduce himself as Carl Hill. He thought it was kind of ironic using the name "Hill." One of the lesser advertised facts about Elmira was the existence of the Elmira Correctional Facility, a maximum security prison known as "the Hill."

Since Carl was paying cash, and paid the first month in advance, no one was asking for proof of identity. No one ever questioned his name. Why would they? If you are introduced to someone who you are told is named Toeslod Doddenpepper you may think it's a bit funny sounding, but your first instinct isn't to call the person a fraud and a liar.

He waited five days before contacting Stan. It was hard to wait, but he made himself do it. He told Stan that he was traveling for his health, but that he would be pleased to work for him again and would be in touch when he got back.

A few days later he drove to Albany and rented a post office box. When he got back to Elmira he also opened a postal box there. He didn't think that anyone could easily watch postal boxes, but he wanted to make sure that if they did watch the one in Albany that they wouldn't see him there.

He waited another two weeks and then went back to Albany and filled out a change of address card to forward any mail he received in Albany to the P.O. Box in Elmira.

It meant paying for two P.O. boxes and a fee every 6 months to renew the order to forward mail from Albany to Elmira, but Carl was careful even then.

Chapter 14

Bought the farm

To die (i.e. insurance money pays off the mortgage) or be knocked out.

They drove both cars back to the office so Joyce could pick up some keys. The property was vacant, so it could be shown without appointment, Joyce explained.

Carl parked his car there and Joyce drove them out to the property. As described, the property fronted on two roads, but neither was a through road and hence there was virtually no traffic on them. Carl noted that the Welland Golf Club was even closer than the airport. That was another plus. The golf club was public; guests at the "spa" could slip over for a round. Carl was already thinking about names. Hot Rock Ranch? Xanadu? Well, perhaps neither of those. It would have to be exclusive and classy.

They drove down both roads to identify the property lines. The parcel of land had roughly 90 degree corners and was about 2,700 feet by 1,900. It had a little extension at the back, a bit like the panhandle of Texas, Carl thought. He was already thinking how that little extension could be used as a folly, or a special wilderness cabin (charge the yokels extra for being farther from the restaurant and tennis courts, he amused himself by thinking.).

The gravel driveway was blocked by a standard square tube farm gate which was secured with a chain and stainless steel lock. Joyce unlocked the gate and they drove into the property. There was a green lapboard frame farmhouse near the gate, a two-story cube with double-hung windows and a porch on two sides. The foundation was cement block, but looked solid. That structure could become the reception area with a little work and retain rustic charm as counterpoint to an ultramodern restaurant. The two functional yet ugly out buildings were behind that. They would have to go.

The property had been set up as a working farm at some point. Then the gravel pit had been discovered and exploited ("developed" would be the business term). After the gravel quarry had either run dry, or ironically more likely hit a spring, it had been abandoned and had become the rather attractive rectangular pond it now was.

Even in its natural state the water was crystal clear. This must be limestone, Carl thought. It would require very little regulation to maintain a sanitary and limpid appearance. The pond was more or less regular in shape and about 300 feet by 200. Carl could see the bottom clearly about thirty feet down. It would be easy to run shielded heat exchange pipes along the bottom and use the natural gas supplies to maintain a comfortable temperature. They could put a retractable cover somewhat like the Sky Dome (oops, Rogers Centre, he corrected himself) to use during the winter or rainy days.

The property had a woodlot of oak and maple which covered about 60 percent of the land. The main part of the woods was open and suitable for walking trails, while the edges were shielded by small pine and hawthorn. Perfect, thought Carl. We could retain most of that and situate the buildings in various positions about the property. I think this could work.

Carl shared some of his thoughts with Joyce and they agreed that someone might very well want to do something here.

"How much would it cost to get it up and running?" Joyce asked him when they were back sitting in her car.

"Quite a lot." Carl responded. "It would take a proper business plan and some expert opinion, and some contractors' estimates to know for sure. But it certainly might make the property saleable just being a possibility."

"When the present owner mentioned the idea I thought it might be just a pipe dream," Joyce said. "But, now I think you're right. It could just work. Thanks for your advice with this."

"No problem. And you know, some of the companies I work with really might be interested."

"Really!"

"Well, we'll see. Let me talk to some of them."

I might be able to make a killing on this place, Carl was amused by thinking. I really do have an odd sense of humor he chided himself. Note to self: be less flippant.

"Oh, about Saturday," he said, "I thought it would be nice to have duck. I found a nice *magret de canard* at Zehrs; we haven't had that for some time. I've also got some nice wine to go with it."

"That would be grand," Joyce agreed. "What made you think of that?"

"I was just remembering that's what we had on our first trip together."

"Still the romantic, aren't you?"

Saturday was a private anniversary they celebrated. It was in mid-September that Carl had proposed to Joyce and they always liked to have a special dinner at about that time to remember it. It had probably been the worst planned and badly executed event of his life.

He had arranged in advance for a ring to be brought in by the waiter with dessert. Joyce had decided she didn't want dessert. He had insisted and they had almost had a fight. Then, when the dessert he had ordered arrived, it turned out that the waiter had forgotten to bring the ring. Carl had to go into the kitchen to retrieve the ring and then try to present it without looking like a complete idiot.

Luckily Joyce saw the funny, not the stupid side of it, and accepted him, warts and all.

Chapter 15

Getting a stake

Whether table stake or entry fee, players have to buy in.

In order to sustain himself without dipping too deeply into his nest egg, Wolf, now Carl Hill, decided that he should look for some employment. He certainly hoped that Stan would actually find a place for him in his stable of assassins. He knew that wasn't the appropriate name for the profession to which he aspired, but he sort of liked the sound of it.

However, it was also possible that Stan might prefer to deal with someone he could look in the eyes.

So, he would need some way to earn some money. Carl examined his job skills: stealing, standing lookout, shooting people, breaking and entering, driving get-away vehicles. Not normally acceptable behavior he had to admit.

Well, maybe the driving would be useful. He could drive a taxi or truck like his old man had sporadically, when not blind drunk. Drink was one vice which had never attracted Carl. He would have a beer with the guys and enjoyed a glass of wine with a meal, but he could take it or leave it. Mostly he didn't like the fact that when you drink you lose control. You lose control of your body, your emotions, and of the situation.

Carl preferred to be in control.

Elmira did not offer a lot of job opportunities for a 23 year old with no official employment history, no mentionable skills, and little formal education.

There was a taxi company. The cabs were all owned by the drivers and what passed for night life in Elmira did not justify having a nightshift driver. Carl asked a few of the guys he found in the local pool hall and learned that some of the wineries north of Elmira hired occasional workers during the harvest and there was a nursery north of the nearby town, Horseheads, which might need a delivery driver.

Harvest apparently started in September, three months away. The people he talked to told him that if nothing else turned up, he would be easily able to get work then because wineries had trouble getting workers. He learned that this was because the hours were long, the work hard, and the period of employment only about six weeks.

He decided to try the nursery. He loved the name Horseheads; it made him think of the scene from The Godfather in which the head of a horse turns up in a bed. How would a town ever get a name like that?

When he went to apply for work he was told that they needed someone to make deliveries to upper New York State, but that it would only be two days per week. That suited Carl. He wasn't looking to become a professional trucker.

Chapter 16

Ducks

The weakest pair one can have is a pair of two's. It is referred to as holding a pair of ducks. Probably this it because they are just waiting to be knocked off. Ironically, having a roast duck can be yummy.

Carl had learned to cook while living on his own. He had learned to love cooking as theyears went by. Now he did most of the cooking for Joyce and him and thought he did a good job of it.

He shopped almost every day and made his choice for dinner based upon what was in season and looked good. He hoped tonight's dinner would meet with approval.

He printed up a menu on his computer. Using restaurant language was so much fun.

Magret de Canard avec champignons savage
Escalope de pommes de terre au four
Salade Verte
Crème Brule a la Orange
Vin: St Peray, Gigondas, Muscat de Beaumes-de-Venise

The trick to cooking duck, Carl believed, was a very hot oven and lots of garlic.

Well, that was one of the important factors. Another was choosing a good piece of Muscovy duck. The black and white pied duck so popular in the Rhone valley of France was, in the opinion of Carl, and many people, the best for roasting.

Of course, the way it was roasted, the spices, the timing, the vegetables it was served with, the sauce, and the wine which accompanied it all counted too.

Carl liked to use the lean breast of the duck, called magret de canard. He had learned from a friend, Michel, in the vineyards of Bordeaux. Michel had shown him how to cut slits at an angle into the skin side of the magret and insert slivers of garlic into each of the little trenches.

After the oven had been raised to 375 degrees, the duck would be roasted with the skin side up to baste the meat with the flavourful fat as it melted away and trickled down over the surface and into the bottom of the pan. The duck itself was lying on a small mesh pedestal to keep it up out of the grease and to allow the heat of the oven to reach it on all sides.

The temperature of the oven would be reduced a little after the duck was showing evidence of being sufficiently seared and was browning nicely.

This evening Carl had decided to roast some wild mushrooms from the selection available at one of their nearby specialty stores. Those would be prepared first with garlic and butter in an iron frying pan and placed in the oven around the duck during the last 15 minutes.

He had also prepared some russet potatoes by slicing them into scallops and parboiling them slightly. Those would also be cooked around the duck. They were to be added just before the mushrooms. As spicing for the vegetables, Carl like to use a prepared vegetable seasoning made by Club House called La Grille which he bought in a largish container at Costco. It was very flavourful while having only 9% salt. Since that was the only salt to be used in the whole meal, he felt its use was justified.

Salad would be served after the main course, in European style. Tonight it would be a variety of lettuces with caramelized almond slivers and a simple olive oil and balsamic vinegar dressing into which he would stir some oregano and orange zest.

The quality of the balsamic vinegar and the olive oil was crucial. Carl was using an aged balsamic vinegar which was quite expensive, but well worth the cost when used sparingly on a fresh salad. His own preference was for a Spanish extra virgin olive oil from the area of Lerida in northern Spain.

Virgin olive oil was as good as Extra Virgin for cooking he believed, but for a salad Extra Virgin was best. Unlike oil labeled simply Olive Oil, both Virgin and Extra Virgin were cold pressed and contain less than one percent acid.

Carl had cheated a little with the Crème Brule. Rather than preparing it from scratch, he had purchased two commercial Crèmes in their individual earthenware pots. But then he hadn't shot his own duck or dug the potatoes out of the ground either. He would add an orange flavoured honey to the custard and caramelize it with the miniature kitchen blow torch Joyce had bought for him for his most recent birthday.

Just before serving, he would decorate the surface with chopped pieces of crystallized orange rind which had been coated in milk chocolate.

He had chosen wines from the Rhone Valley to accompany the food.

As in everything else, Carl believed in taking care and paying attention to details.

Chapter 17

Checking the Pot

A decision to go in (i.e. call) may be based on how big the pot is compared to the required bet.

The boarding house Carl had chosen, run by Mrs. Clark, was cheap and cheerful. Well, it was more cheap than cheerful. There was a place to park his car around back and there were only two other people staying there.

Best of all, the other boarders were there more or less permanently. Carl thought it highly unlikely that anyone he knew would come to Elmira at all, much less stay at Clark's boarding house. But the less chance of an outsider meeting Carl, the better he felt.

Carol, a young school teacher, had been there for nine months. She was just completing her first year of teaching grade school at the nearby elementary school, Arthur W Booth. The other boarder, Timothy, was a middle aged law clerk at Morgan, Morgan, and Morgan, a prominent local law firm with an office near the Chemung County Courthouse. Both walked to work early each morning and Mrs. Clark was not the sort to pry into another person's privacy, so Carl was not required to deal with much in the way of explanations.

Mrs. Clark may have had, probably did have, a first name, but Carl never heard it spoken. She was always 'Mrs. Clark'. A woman one would describe as handsome, she walked with an erect posture which made her seem tall. She was in fact two inches shorter than Carl's 5' 9", but it was only when he was standing very near her that he realized that she was not as tall as he. She was probably in her mid-fifties, but Carl suspected that she was a person who would carry her age well. Her family history was not offered, nor did Carl believe that inquiry would be welcome. That suited him fine since he was not into sharing.

Carol was pretty, in a quiet, mousey sort of way. Timothy was mousey, but not as quiet.

Timothy preferred to be called "Timothy," not "Tim." Carl suspected that at some time he had been teased as "Tiny Tim." He was short, even 3 or 4 inches shorter than Carl. He was also quite slight, some would say skinny. He actually was Tiny Tim.

The food was simple home cooking in reasonable portions. Judging by a number of archival menus he had found on one corner of the reading desk they all shared in the parlor, the fare tended to repeat itself with some seasonal variation. A typical week seemed to be a roast chicken on Sunday, chicken pot pie Monday, spaghetti Tuesday, ham Wednesday, shepherd's pie on Thursday, breaded fish on Friday, and pork chops with cabbage Saturday.

Although it was called a boarding house, they all took only two meals there per day. Breakfast was always a boiled egg or cereal, toast with homemade jam, orange juice and coffee. The other two boarders ate their lunch near where they worked and

Carl was happy enough to pick up something wherever he happened to be.

Carl had done a bit of cooking since his mother had been killed. He cooked mostly for himself. Usually his father didn't care whether he ate or not; often he was too drunk to bother.

Because he had grown up in a neighbourhood with a wide ethnic mix, Carl had eaten a bit of everything by the time he was twenty. Many times he had eaten at the homes of friends and he had acquired a very catholic taste in food.

Italian dishes of all types, from polenta to gnocchi, were served in the various homes he visited. All the dishes were homemade; all the wines were too, at least half the time. He tasted wine first when he was ten and learned early to drink in moderation. Italian was still one of his favorite cuisines. Risotto with mushrooms and linguini with scallops were favorites, but he enjoyed any well prepared Italian meal.

There were Indians and Pakistanis among his playmates and he had eaten both curried beef madras and butter chicken before he knew what they were called. A sister of one of his friends had shown him how easy it was to make naan bread and he adored the blend of citric oils and chilies in the lime pickle condiments.

The children of Eastern European families who had joined the melting pot of America introduced perogies and cabbage rolls. He still remembered first tasting pepperoni with ketchup on crusty white bread which a young Czech shared with him.

One of the few other German families had their influence on his epicurean development as well. Although he wasn't sure how to make them, he loved the potato pancakes and schnitzel which he tasted when he visited.

With such a broad experience to good foods of the world while still young, it was no surprise that Carl found the boarding house food a bit tame. As soon as possible he would look for an apartment which would allow him to cook for himself.

Chapter 18

Table stakes

In a Table Stakes game, players can only bet what they have on the table.

Carl spent most of Saturday at the market and in the kitchen. He had printed off the menu and glued it into a folded piece of blue construction paper. On the front he attached a picture of the Pont d'Avignon. Their first trip to Europe had been to France. During their second trip to France they had visited Avignon, a southern Rhone town encircled by magnificent crenellated walls

It was early July in the midst of the annual drama festival. Their hotel was a small 15th century building on the main square, the Place de l'Horloge. Carl had reserved four months in advance and had been fortunate to get such a good location. From their hotel window they could watch a variety of buskers in the main square. The hotel restaurant was open on two sides to the warm summer breeze. A short adjoining passageway brought them to the open court in front of the Palais des Papes, the home of the seven Popes who presided during the period between 1309 and 1378 when the Catholic Church had two Popes, one in Rome and one in Avignon.

Joyce had loved the hotel with its spiral staircase of yellow stone. They had spent two wonderful weeks there and visited Roman sites in the area.

They climbed the tiers of the Roman arena in Nimes and watched young boys practicing the art of bullfighting on the sand below. They visited the Pont de Gard and marveled at the huge three levels of stone arches support for the aqueduct which is believed to have been constructed 2,000 years ago by the Roman General Agrippa.

They enjoyed lunches in villages and sampled local wines. One of the dishes they had enjoyed most was the breast of duck served with Gigondas or Cotes du Rhone Village wine.

One cloudless day they had stood on the ruins of the ancient summer house of the Popes in the nearby town of Chateauneuf du Pape and toasted love and life with glasses of the wine made there which takes its name from the town.

As his computer desktop screen, Carl had a treasured photograph of them standing atop the windswept Roman garrison which guarded the pass at Gap.

Tonight's menu was intended as a reminder of those happy days and a celebration of their life together.

As they sat gazing out across the river, Joyce said "Whenever anyone mentions France, I think of our trip to Avignon. I'm glad I saw it first with you."

"I am too," Carl responded. "And Italy, and Spain."

"Yes, those places too. But, it was in France that I saw how romantic you are."

They sat quietly for a few more minutes sipping the Muscat de Beaumes-de-Venise dessert wine which they had enjoyed first together in the Rhone town of that name. Then, by common accord, they rose and went to bed where they lay in each others arms for a long time reminding each other of other places they had been together after France and making plans for future journeys.

They had liked each other from their first meeting in Cuba. They had fallen in love over the next few months in the most natural progression.

Naturally, the first time they had slept together had been very special.

But as they made love this night it was deep, and slow and gentle, with the shared intensity which only comes with mutual love and understanding. They fell asleep still touching each other and woke to a clear, blue sky.

Life together was good.

Soon Carl would contact Stan for the last time.

Chapter 19

How much have I invested?

If a player has already put a lot into a pot, staying in may make sense.

Saturday night together had been wonderful, especially the part which came after they had finished their dessert wine and gone upstairs. Carl felt as if he were at the beginning of life, not half way through.

They had been married for fifteen years and Carl hoped they would have another fifteen as good. We'll take it fifteen years at a time, he thought.

He thought again about Stan. No hurry there. He would call from a public phone in the U.S. when he went over to clear out the P.O. Box there for the last time ever. Probably he could do that Tuesday before poker.

He wanted to go across to get some special cheese at Premier Cheese and Liquor. After talking about how good the cheese in Europe was, Carl wanted to buy some cheese from Italy, France and Spain for snacks at poker. Normally each of the visiting players brought one or two snack foods to share so the host for the night didn't have to take care of that. Maybe he could find some Gorgonzola, Bleu d'Auvergne, and Manchego

Usually he heard from Stan four or five times per year. Right now Stan was probably thinking of anything but Carl. He'd be surprised when Carl called him.

He would also be surprised at Carl's decision to retire. Stan had seemed old to Carl in the 70s, but he must have only been about 30. Stan would still be in his 50s, Carl thought. Still a young man. Funny how one's perception of age changes with one's own aging.

Monday he took a run down to Chippawa to check on his boat. In a few weeks he would want to consider removing it from the water. The season was a lot shorter here than in Bermuda, where he would prefer to have a boat. But as long as their main house was in Ontario, it made no sense to have a boat elsewhere.

As it was, he used the boat about ten times per year. A boat is a hole in the water into which you pour money, he reminded himself. Still they enjoyed it from time to time and it was one of his few extravagances.

He had bought the boat in a moment of madness probably. The name, painted on the stern was *Reflections*. He had considered changing her name, but by the time he had looked into the arcane rites which tradition demanded for propitious altering of a boat's name, he had grown used to *Reflections*. She was a 26 foot Chris Craft with a 9 and one-half foot beam. That made for a very roomy interior for a boat of that length. The 350 hp V8 inboard/outboard was about average in absurdly high fuel consumption and she cruised nicely at about 26 knots. Some said that if you were going to spend your time motoring above the Falls you needed to have two motors. Drifting over the Falls was not a pleasant prospect.

Carl had devised his own solution. He installed a very large anchor, an 18 kg Plow and set it up on a pulpit such that it could be launched in a moment by releasing a simple restraint. That anchor, attached as it was to a seventy-foot rode, would hold a much larger boat than his, even in the Niagara River current. Even two engines could fail. Fuel lines could foul. A good anchor with a strong rode would always work. Carl had an eclectic mind. Often it helped him think outside the box. Other times it just free associated. Hope is the Anchor of my Soul, he thought.

He had considered having the boat moved by trailer to a marina below the Falls for next season. It might be fun to go over to Toronto by water some time. He would talk to Joyce about the idea. Life was good.

Joyce had been very excited about the Welland farm land parcel. She even mentioned it before dinner Saturday night. She had put an ad in the local papers and someone from Lewiston, NY had called the office to talk with her about it. She had been out of the office in one of the dead zones which occur in numerous locations around the Niagara peninsula and her cell phone was out of contact. She had returned the call later but had not found anyone home.

She asked Carl again if his business contacts actually might be interested and he said he wanted to also mention it to one or two of the guys Tuesday night.

Chapter 20

I'll Pass

To abstain from betting, to check, sometimes used to mean to drop out.

When he arrived for poker, which was being held at Dave's place this week, he took the opportunity to raise the spa idea with Dave. If anyone could put the numbers together to find out if it was worthwhile or not, it was Dave. Carl knew that Dave's brother was an architect with contacts in construction and between the three of them they might be able to do a cost/profit estimate without spending much.

Perhaps Dave and a few friends would be interested in an investment.

"It does sound interesting," Dave said, after Carl laid out the general idea. "The major problem for me at the moment would be financing. But, you know I would like to branch out on my own. Working for the county is mind numbing."

Dave had been the financial officer for the Niagara region for 15 years. He was always complaining that politics kept getting in the way of sound financial planning.

The game seemed strangely slow. Carl's cards were so bad they were good. They kept him out of pots where he would have lost. The game ground on and the impatient players pushed ahead and took themselves out.

Before long Carl found himself in third position with only three players remaining. He had played very few hands and had won one or two small pots. But he was still in the game. Dave had a little more than him, and Terry, of all people, was chip leader by a long shot. There was a lesson here. Sometimes all you have to do is keep on keeping on.

The very next hand Carl found two aces as his down cards. He made a small raise and Dave, who usually was very conservative in his play went all-in. Well, if you don't call with a pair of aces before the flop, when would you call, Carl asked himself.

Carl confidently called the all-in and Dave flipped up a pair of kings. When Carl showed his aces, Dave slapped his forehead and propped his head on his two hands.

Tom was taking his turn at dealing and laid out the flop for them. Two 3's and a ten changed nothing except it made Carl's aces look even safer. On the turn Tom laid out a third 3 which gave both Dave and Carl tights, but left Carl with the almost sure lock. The only card that could win for Dave would be a king.

So, Carl felt less surprise than one might imagine when a king showed up on the river.

Here was another lesson. Sometimes odds don't mean shit.

Carl took over the dealing from Tom and a few hands later Dave overtook Terry and won the stakes.

"Nice river, I thought," Dave said, rubbing it in just a bit as they sat over a beer beside his fireplace.

"I should have just folded the aces," Carl replied. "Everyone knows aces don't hold up."

"I always prefer calling with a low pair," Tom joined in. "That way you can only improve."

"I've noticed you do that, Tom," Dave retorted. "That's why I always call you."

"I could count on one hand the number of times you've called me this year," Tom shot back. He was probably right, Carl thought.

"Would you two take it outside, please? Some of us are trying to forget about poker," Terry told them. Terry had been in control of the game until the last few minutes. He seldom finished in the top two and had thought tonight was his chance to win it all.

Dave moved over to sit beside Carl and asked "If this retreat development opportunity is as good as you think it is, how many partners would you consider?"

"Well, the corporate group I work with would want at least 50 percent. The other 50 percent could be cut up anyway at all. But I would think that three or four would be the best mix. If you have too many partners, you might as well go public," Carl told him.

"And we're probably looking at between 3 and 4 million to get this rolling, right?"

"Yes," Carl replied carefully. "Pending a more accurate estimate."

"We could get about 80 percent financing," Dave said. "That would mean raising at least $800,000. If you put up $400,000, I could scrape together $100,000. I couldn't come up with more cash right now," Dave added, "but I've got a friend stateside who is always looking for investments. I could give him a call if you like. I've known him for some years and know he's got good connections."

"I'd like to keep this local as much as possible," Carl countered.

"Steve is about as local as you can be and still be in the U.S.," Dave answered. "He's right across the border in Lewiston."

Carl didn't say anything, but he started wondering if he really wanted to pursue this idea. It was well known that some people living in the mansions along the riverside near Lewiston had some connections he would rather avoid.

As he drove slowly toward home, he remembered that Joyce had already received a phone enquiry from Lewiston. Maybe he'd better pull in his horns.

Chapter 21

Kicker

Backup card to the main hand (eg. 10's and 4's with an ace kicker).

Joyce was asleep when Carl crawled into bed next to her. She stirred and asked sleepily "Who won?"

"Dave," he responded. "He got lucky. My luck dried up."

Joyce probably hadn't even heard the end of his response. She was sleep-breathing already.

Carl was not feeling sleepy. He was thinking of Dave's mention of money from an outside source and the enquiry Joyce's advertisement had generated. Was he being paranoid? Yes, probably he was. Although, hadn't it been said that when you know there are people who would like you dead, you had better be sure you are paranoid enough.

He had spent the last 25 years being careful. This was not the time to stop keeping his guard up and his head down.

Tomorrow he would tell Joyce that his investors group had decided against the spa project and he'd phone Dave to tell him the same. Joyce could still sell the property to someone whether or not they developed it for some commercial purpose. Maybe one of the overpaid and under performing bank CEOs would buy the land to create a private estate. Some of them could do that with the salary they were paid for one year of bad decisions.

That decided, Carl fell into a fitful sleep which was crowded with a variety of dreams involving characters who resembled Robert DeNiro and Joe Pesci.

There was one scene that always seemed to pop up in Carl's troubled dreams. It would suddenly occur out of context and always by surprise. He would be looking for something, or someone, or he would be coming into a room or around a corner, suddenly he would see someone he knew. Their eyes would lock and he would be unable to look away. Sometimes he would jerk awake to break the contact. Other times he would try to run but his feet would refuse to move.

Sometimes when he had that dream, or rather that episode in a dream, he would wake to find his legs wrapped up in the bedding, or Joyce would wake him to tell him to stop kicking.

He had mentioned his kicking in his sleep to his doctor and a test had been done to check the level of iron in his blood. Go figure, he thought; it's like the character in the story by Dickens. The suggestion was that the cause of a bad dream could be something one had eaten. Now here was his own doctor checking chemical levels for the same phenomena.

His iron level was found to be normal and he thought no more about it. Everyone has bad dreams occasionally, he imagined.

Carl slept badly and had trouble waking up at his usual early hour. Finally he awoke to find Joyce already downstairs preparing coffee. He showered and went down in his housecoat to find her hurrying to leave for the office.

"Wish me luck," she called out as she headed out the front door. "I've got a meeting with a prospective buyer."

"Luck!" he called after her. He couldn't help wondering if the meeting concerned the spa property and a Mafioso. Now you are being obsessive, he thought. It's not all about you.

Chapter 22

Over card

A higher card that, if matched, could win (e.g., you have Kings but an Ace comes up on the board).

It was all very well calling himself Carl here in Elmira, but he needed to set up a cover that would prevent anyone tracking him down. Maybe Stan would never offer him another contract, but in case he did, Carl wanted to be ready.

He had always enjoyed reading and knew that a public library could be a source of information. Now he began looking at ways that money could be moved around legally and what was involved in changing one's name.

His truck driving often took him near several of the university towns and he discovered that even without entry requirements he could take non-credit courses.

He soon learned in one of the courses that what passed as normal business practices provided plenty of opportunities to hide money, or at least to move it about. There were lots of accounts of how businesses set up offshore banking and how corporations declared profits in countries of choice to minimize taxes. There were even shipping lines who registered their ships in landlocked countries because it was cheaper.

Corporations were treated by the law as if they were individual persons. His teacher, who had a jaundiced view of business in general, told the class that corporations had originally been set up mainly to shield dishonest businessmen from prosecution. He explained that while corporations had the power to sue and could be sued, the board of directors could not easily be held personally responsible.

By way of example, Carl's instructor outlined the role of the board of directors in the many deaths which had occurred from exploding Pintos. The small car had a design flaw in the placement and protection of its gas tank. In disturbingly large numbers, they tended to burst into flames when hit from behind. A significant number of people were trapped inside the burning cars and died horribly. The defect could be corrected, but it would be expensive for Ford to recall and repair all the Pintos they had sold.

Ford ran a cost analysis which determined that it would be much cheaper for the corporation to leave the cars as they were and make out-of-court settlements with the estates of the people thus killed. Of course, it would be criminal to knowingly allow people to die to maximize profits, but a defensible explanation was devised.

Ford argued that if they issued a recall, each of the owners of the Pintos would have to drive to the Ford service centres to have the repairs made. By totaling up the number of extra miles to be driven and using probability tables, Ford argued that the additional driving would potentially cause additional deaths. So, the corporation left the defective cars on the road and continued to make out-of-court settlements.

Carl wondered briefly if he could set up a corporate hit man and be merely the CEO of the corporation. He didn't think courts would buy that since he would still be the one pulling the trigger.

Still, he could see how the corporate structure might distance him from the money being exchanged. It would also make it easier to hide his residence and make the contact between him and Stan more nebulous.

It was also possible to use a limited company to set up a bank account to make it less obvious that a payment made by a corporation was actually going to him.

He could even set up a corporation and use that corporate name as if it where his own name. The possibility of becoming Carl Hill Inc. amused him.

Then he discovered that he could legally change his name fairly easily.

Timothy, his fellow boarder at Mrs. Clark's, introduced him to one of the junior lawyers at Morgan, Morgan, and Morgan. It wasn't one of the Morgan's.

Timothy had a joke. It was his only joke as far as Carl knew. Timothy told it to Carl within a few days of meeting him. Carol asked him a week or so later if Timothy had told Carl "his" joke. She seemed in no doubt about what joke he would tell.

The joke was long, at least the way Timothy told it. It amounted to the following:

A client phones the law office.

A man answers, "Morgan, Morgan, and Morgan."

"May I speak to Mr. Morgan?"

"Mr. Morgan passed away some years ago."

"Oh, I'm sorry. Could I speak to Mr. Morgan then?"
"Mr. Morgan is in court all day today."
"Well, in that case could I speak to Mr. Morgan?"
"Speaking!"

"Lord love a duck, if that isn't a thigh-slapper," Carl was tempted to exclaim, but he didn't need to offend Timothy. He smiled politely and said, "I never saw that coming."

The lawyer Carl consulted explained that since he had no criminal record he could apply for a name change just based upon the unfortunate inconvenience posed by the name Wolfgang Amadeus Hiltz. For a small fee, it was done. Carl Hill was his future; W.A. Hiltz was history.

Chapter 23

Judgment call

Sometimes you have to estimate if your hand is good enough.

Am I a bad person? Every once in a while, especially now that he had turned 46 and was either approaching, or moving beyond, middle age, Carl asked himself that.

He knew that most people, probably all judges and most juries, would conclude that he was bad. But did that mean it was true? Stan would say he was a good hit man, but perhaps Stan would mean proficient rather than good in a moral sense.

Robin Hood was an outlaw; but he was also regarded as a hero for the oppressed.

Granted, Carl didn't steal from the rich and give to the poor. He received money from the rich and killed the person the rich person fingered. That made him more like the sheriff of Nottingham than like Robin Hood, he concluded.

Was the sheriff of Nottingham a bad person? Well, nobody liked him. He was no hero. According to the stories he wasn't even very good at his job.

On the other hand...

I'm good to children and animals, Carl thought. I'm a good husband to Joyce. He had always been faithful and truthful with Joyce except for not being completely forthcoming about how he earned his money. It wasn't that he lied. He just downplayed the part about shooting people.

Real estate people skate close to the truth too, he would wager. He'd seen the way they described property they were tying to sell; if that wasn't lying, it was the next thing to it.

I pay my taxes; mostly, he amended. I certainly pay enough.

I obey most laws. I stop at red lights. I don't speed. I've never been convicted of a major crime and I've never shot anyone by accident. I usually leave a tip and am polite to wait people. A jury of wait staff would like him. He'd have to tell his lawyer that if he ended up in court.

I try to use politically correct language, such as saying "wait people".

Okay, so once in a while I whack someone. Is that so bad? Society is better off because I've killed the people I kill, he rationalized.

How did he compare to the loan sharks and phony financial advisers that drove people to suicide or worse by squeezing them for money? Money is not evil in itself, the bible teaches; it is the love of money which is the root of all evil.

I may not be good; but, am I evil?

Carl wasn't religious by nature. He could see why many people were, it just didn't work for him. If there is a God he thought, God can sort out the good from the evil.

But, speaking of being religious, hadn't there been a group of warrior monks?

Thinking of that got him thinking about how some people pronounce "guerrilla" as if it were "gorilla." Then that got him picturing armed apes. And that reminded him of a T-shirt he'd seen at a gun show that had a picture of a polar bear with a Tommy gun. The caption was "Support your right to keep and arm bears."

Carl did support the right of bears, and other victims of hunting, to be armed. Maybe he could do some pro bono work offering protection for flocks of ducks, or providing covering fire for herds of deer as they scampered to safety. That might earn him some Karma points.

People ride around on elephants shooting at tigers; but, let a tiger eat even one hunter and people start complaining and calling him a "man-eating" tiger.

In Spain they call the one who finishes off the bull with a sword a matador, which quite literally means "killer". Maybe if he had business cards printed calling himself a matador, people would not judge him so harshly.

That made him decide that maybe "Good" and "Evil" were concepts that no one could really judge.

Chapter 24

Suits me

Aside from the common meaning, it indicates getting a card in the suit you need, for example, to fill a flush.

Driving a truck was not so bad, as long as you didn't have to do it full-time, Carl concluded. Full-time it would be boring. Maybe that was why his father drank so much.

He had five days off each week and he used that time to catch up on the things he had neglected to learn in school. Then it had been uncool; now it was information he wanted and needed.

He read widely and made plans.

The nursery didn't insist that he come back the same day he made a delivery. As long as he didn't abuse the privilege and there was no rush order for the following day, they let him use the truck to stop off at classes he attended.

He always topped up the tank if he drove extra miles on personal business and the nursery took note of that and approved.

When he contacted Stan again, he had his structure in place. He told Stan that he was prepared to finance hits himself and accept payment upon successful completion.

That surprised Stan. Usually agents demanded at least half up front and asked for expenses.

Carl had thought it through. He could probably demand a higher fee by taking it after the fact, and he didn't want to submit an expense claim. He didn't want anyone to know what he did, where he stayed, or how he traveled.

He knew that as a new agent it was up to him to prove himself, and he believed in himself. This way Stan was risking nothing. If Carl got himself killed, Stan was out nothing.

He had decided to conserve his money so as to make it possible for him to remain independent. He had learned from his business studies that the most important thing in business was to keep overhead as low as possible so as to be able to live through slack times.

Carl could just about cover his daily expenses from what he earned as a truck driver. He conserved his money. He didn't smoke, he didn't drink, and he lived simply at the boarding house. His greatest expenditure was for his studies and books.

Carl, who always remained Wolf as far as Stan was concerned, also wanted payment through a safe conduit. That was easier to demand after he had successfully completed the contract.

With his new-found understanding of business terminology, Carl found it interesting that the very proper term "contract" was applied to what was a totally illegal action. It would be hard to imagine arguing in a court of law that the hitter had, in accordance with contractual agreement, hit the target and was thus entitled to payment as promised.

But, if Carl was going to work as a hired gun, he wanted it to be on his terms.

He wanted to be able to turn down hits which were either too dangerous or were morally repugnant. He wouldn't object to hitting a loan shark or a thug, but he would not just kill whoever he was pointed at.

Was that possible? Could he kill selectively? Would Stan go along with that?

Carl didn't know, but he would find out. Carl had standards of right and wrong. They might not be as snow white as those some people had, but they were his.

He also wanted to set up a way to hide some of the money he was paid and to pay some to himself through a legitimate front. Isn't that called an oxymoron, he wondered? If it's a front, how can it be legitimate?

Well, whatever one called it, he wanted to ensure that there was no easy way to connect him to the hit.

Carl was enjoying what he was learning about business. The more he learned, the more he came to think that the line between legal and illegal was a matter of opinion. If your lawyers could outwit the other lawyers you were innocent; if not you were guilty.

"If the glove don't fit, you must acquit" wasn't that the joke his generation had grown up with? Some people thought a man was guilty; some thought he was innocent. But usually a rich person with good lawyers was more likely to get off than a poor one.

Chapter 25

Deal me in

A request to be included in a game or hand.

Carl had been thinking about how he should approach Stan about calling it quits. On the face of it, that seemed easy enough. He was paid by piecework rather than a retainer. Still he wanted to leave on good terms. One thing he wanted Stan to know was that he wasn't going to work with, or for, someone else.

Stan had always been good to work with. He had been very cooperative about the corporate bank account money transfers, whereas that might have seemed odd to him.

On the other hand, maybe that was normal procedure these days. Hell, if movies like Casino were anything to go by perhaps it was more of a legit business.

On the other hand, he'd heard that with the Russian Mafia and the Triads, things were becoming rougher.

Hell, the truth was, Carl didn't really know anything about how organized crime worked. He was just a guy they called in to clean up things from time to time. He neither knew about nor cared about internal politics. Carl didn't even know much about disorganized crime. He hadn't been involved for more than twenty years.

Probably your average CEO was more involved in day-to-day crime than Carl was. If the reports about Enron, Conrad Black, and Madoff were to be believed, most CEOs seemed to be flaunting the law left and right.

Carl was lost in thoughts like these when the phone rang at 10:30.

"Hello," Carl said. He didn't mean anything by it. It was just a thing he said when he answered the phone.

"Hi, lover," Joyce said playfully. "Boy, were you right!"

"What, again?"

"Yep, I finally got in touch with that prospective buyer from Lewiston yesterday evening after you left for poker."

At the word Lewiston Carl felt as if a hand was squeezing his heart. He knew it was irrational, but coming as it did while thinking about Stan and after his talk with Dave, and the associated dreams he had last night...

"And . . .?" he asked inquisitively.

"And he's interested," she bubbled. "He was just here. He thinks your ideas are great. In fact he wants to meet you to discuss the project."

"Well, as far as that goes, I've had some talks with the investors I work with and they're very cool on the idea," he said, trying not to sound too serious.

"Oh, but you were so optimistic."

She sounded so disappointed that he hurried to explain. "It's not that they don't like the idea. It's just that development money is tight right now. You know how nervous the recent economic problems have made everyone."

"Yes, but if you could meet with my client and just explain some of the ideas you had. I'm sure he's interested. He might even want to hire you to work with him on the project."

What could he say? He was the one who had got her excited about the idea. What could it hurt just to meet this guy and discuss a few ideas? It might even lead to some more conventional work, more along the lines of what he'd been claiming to do all along.

"Sure," he said, "I'd be happy to meet with him. Is he there now?"

"He had to rush off. But I gave him our number and he said he'd call you later today," Joyce said. "I hope that's okay."

"Of course," Carl reassured her. "I was planning to do some research on-line today anyway. I'll be around here all day."

"Thank you so much for this. I'll be home early today myself. I've got a showing, but it's scheduled for 2:00 and I don't expect it to take long," she told him. "I'll see you."

She hung up and Carl leaned back in his chair and tried to examine how he felt. Okay. He thought, so this guy lives in Lewiston; does that mean that he's a threat? Maybe the time for you to quit is overdue when a little thing like this upsets you so much.

He'd talk to the guy. Share some ideas. Help Joyce sell the property. No big deal. Try to get a hold of yourself, Carl. Next thing you'll be checking the house for listening devices and claiming that the lunar landing was filmed in Sudbury. You're not nervous about Don Ziraldo because of his first name, are you?

Chapter 26

Wild Card

Usually only found in non-serious games, a card that could be anything.

At 2:15 the phone rang. Carl looked at it closely, picked it up gingerly, and offered a guarded "Hello."

"Mr. Hill?" a voice inquired.

"Yes," he admitted.

"Please allow me to introduce myself. My name is Rizzo, Mario Rizzo. Your wife said I could phone you this afternoon. I hope I'm not disturbing you?"

"Not at all," he lied. "I was just doing some reading, but I was expecting your call."

"Well I hope it's not an imposition. I met with your wife this morning and looked at the property for sale near the airport. You know the one I mean?"

"Yes," Carl said. "She told me that you might call. How can I help you?" I certainly hope we can do this over the phone, he thought. That would suit me best.

"Well, your wife told me of some of the ideas you had for how a resort could be set up on that land. I like the idea very much. She told me that you do business consulting. I'd be pleased to meet with you to discuss this project and if we find we can work together, perhaps that might lead to something larger which might be profitable for you."

Just exactly what I'd like to avoid, Carl almost said.

How can I avoid this without screwing things up for Joyce? He could think of no way to gracefully refuse to meet. Unless...

"Mr. Rizzo, I'm happy to discuss some ideas I had, but I'm not really an expert at this part of business. Perhaps if you could give me your e-mail I could sketch out some ideas and send them to you without any obligation on your part. I've really got more work than I can easily handle in other projects right now, but I'd be happy to send you the thoughts I had about this property."

There was a silence on the line. It was not long, but it was noticeable. When Mr. Rizzo spoke again there was a trace of formality in the tone. "Of course, Mr. Hill. I understand that you have other business to attend to. As to e-mail, well I am a bit old-fashioned, I'm afraid. I prefer to do things in person. I have a proposal. I have a meeting this afternoon in St. Catharines and will be returning through Niagara Falls to pick up some papers your wife is preparing for me. Perhaps you and your wife would agree to be my guests for dinner. I could pick up the papers then and we could discuss your ideas over a meal."

It's a trap, don't go, Carl's imagination shrieked. In fact, it was a lot better than him going to some lonely mansion in Lewiston or Mr. Rizzo coming to their home. "I'd have to check with Joyce, Mr. Rizzo, but that sounds like a nice idea," he said through gritted teeth.

"Please do not trouble yourself, Mr. Hill. I will need to contact her in any case to arrange to pick up the papers. If it is agreeable with you, I will suggest that we meet at Casa Mia for dinner at 7:00. Do you know where it is?" His voice had regained its smooth character. He's someone who is used to getting his way, Carl realized.

"Yes, I do. That would be very nice." Carl and Joyce had eaten a couple times at Casa Mia. It was one of the Niagara Falls' restaurants which was not spoiled by being in a tourist area. A bit upscale for the $4.99 breakfast crowd, he imagined. He had enjoyed looking over their wine list the last time they'd eaten there. Someone on the staff took a real interest in wines. It could be the owner, since he seemed always there and Carl had seen him occasionally bringing a special bottle to a table.

"Very good, that's all arranged then. I shall call you back only if there is some alteration." The phone went dead and Carl found he was gripping the phone so tightly that his hand had cramped a bit.

He got up and walked into the kitchen. Since dining room, kitchen, and living room stretched along the rear of the house, he could look out across the river as he poured himself a coffee. Somewhere across there is the house of Mr. Rizzo, he thought. I wonder if it is in view. He decided that none of the houses which backed on the bank opposite their own looked grand enough. He pictured Mr. Rizzo in a walled estate with a large curving driveway filled with black cars with tinted windows.

He had noticed that he could not think of Mr. Rizzo as Mario. He certainly had an air of formality about him.

The phone sounded and Carl walked into the living room to pick up that extension.

"Carl," Joyce sounded a little tense. "I just spoke with Mr. Rizzo." Aha, thought Carl, probably only Mr. Rizzo's mother ever called him Mario.

"Yes," he replied. "So did I."

"He told me that we are going to meet for dinner together," she said. "I hope you don't mind. I hate dragging you into my work like this."

"Not at all, I was the one who started talking about developing that property. It's no big deal," he told her. "What is he like?"

"Oh, he seems nice enough. He's quite formal, but charming too."

"Well, don't worry about it. I'll put a few ideas on paper and we will enjoy ourselves," he assured her. As least I hope so, he thought in an aside.

"Okay. I'll be home soon."

Carl thought about how nice it would be to be sitting on a sunny hillside in Spain eating olives and Manchego cheese and sipping sherry or Malaga wine.

Chapter 27

Ante up

A request that a player put in an amount to participate. In Texas Hold'em two players, small blind and large blind, put in an ante. Toward the end of a tournament game, all remaining players may have to ante.

Five weeks after he arrived in Elmira, Carl was starting to relax. He had money in the bank. He'd found out how he could change his name legally. His course at the university in Buffalo had shown him how he could set up a safe way to be paid. He had worked out a way that Stan could contact him without knowing where he was.

Then it occurred to him that he might be taking too much for granted.

Maybe Stan wouldn't want to do business this way.

He should contact Stan again and find out.

He was near Buffalo a few days later on a delivery. He drove to the airport and went into the arrivals area. Maybe he was being too cautious he cautioned himself. Then he made a decision which he would try to follow for the rest of his life: "Don't worry about being too careful; worry about not being careful enough."

His idea, which he thought was kind of clever, was that he would check arrivals and mention casually to Stan that he just got back in the area. He wouldn't mention where he was flying in from or where he was, but he would count on background noise to establish atmosphere.

He found a pay phone in a noisy area and obtained a large quantity of change.

Stan answered right away and the conversation went well. They were both guarded in the wording of their conversation and Carl made a point of mentioning that he was at an airport.

Stan confirmed his continued interest in employing Carl and even said he thought he might have something suitable. He told Carl that it would be something minor, but it would pay well.

They arranged that Stan would drop him a line.

Stan asked where Carl had been and Carl was vague but mentioned that the weather down south was good and he'd enjoyed getting a little sun.

As he walked back to the truck, Carl felt excited and optimistic. The future looked bright.

He drove back to Elmira with ideas swimming in his head. Where would this offer Stan had take him? How would he travel? If he had to fly, how could he take a gun?

He put those thoughts to the back of his mind as he drove into the nursery loading area. He had met one of the secretaries from the office and they were going to a dance in town.

Chapter 28

I'll see you

Meaning I'll match your bet; show me your cards.

When Joyce got home she was her usual cheery self. Carl tried to match her mood, but he had a really bad feeling about meeting Mr. Rizzo.

Carl wasn't religious and he thought that should also mean he shouldn't be superstitious.

In general he wasn't. If a black cat crossed in front of him, he said "Hi Kitty" and kept on walking. He didn't have a lucky number. In his experience bad things didn't happen in threes; they came in any number and it was up to you to take steps to change them.

Yes, sometimes one was lucky, but mostly one had to make one's own luck.

Also, what many people called being unlucky was just not preparing well enough. He remembered a flight instructor friend once telling him something he took to heart. The pilot had said, "A good pilot isn't surprised when something goes wrong on takeoff; he's surprised when it doesn't."

Carl drove defensively. He checked his blind spot before changing lanes. He cleaned and oiled his guns, and he used his own form of checklist before embarking on something potentially dangerous.

He didn't think he had ever heard of anyone named Rizzo, except Dustin Hoffman in Midnight Cowboy, and he had no reason to expect that Mr. Rizzo had ever heard of him.

But, and this was a big but, he remembered the saying: "You lie down with dogs and you can expect to get fleas."

Carl had always avoided places where gangsters, for want of a better word, might congregate.

There was a reason movies always depicted characters such as Tony Soprano in strip joints and with prostitutes. Hell's Angels may be harmless if you leave them alone, but if you crash one of their parties or try to rip them off for drugs, you're going to find trouble.

Maybe Mr. Rizzo was just an honest businessman whose name happened to end in a vowel. But why take chances?

Joyce suggested a cocktail before they changed for dinner. Carl mixed her a Cosmo and settled for a Virgin Caesar for himself. It was time to keep his mind straight and his powder dry, to coin a phrase.

Chapter 29

A card mechanic

A term indicating that a player can manipulate cards to cheat.

Casa Mia is a one-story, tempura stucco structure set back appropriately from the road on Portage Avenue. It has a reputation for good food, good service, a pleasant décor and ambiance and prices which go with that. It offers good value for good money.

We don't always get what we pay for, Carl thought. But we seldom get more than we pay for. That made him remember another cliché: "sometimes we get more than we bargained for".

Carl was driving his car. He turned carefully into the parking lot. There was a black Mercedes parked toward the back of the parking area. Aha, Carl thought.

"There's Mr. Rizzo's car," Joyce told him.

Carl was surprised to find Joyce pointing out a very nicely restored Austin Healey 3000.

"That looks like a 1958 or '59," Carl said in amazement.

"He told me that he's had it for years. He does a lot of the maintenance himself apparently."

Carl did a little reality check with himself. This didn't sound like the sort of hobby one would expect of a mafia kingpin. Perhaps he had Mr. Rizzo all wrong.

"What sort of business is he in?" Carl asked, trying to sound casual.

"Construction, I think," Joyce answered. "I left his business card in my card file in my car. But, it lists various construction-related activities."

At least he's not a meat packer, Carl thought. There were many reasons Carl didn't eat hot dogs or bologna. Carl gave himself a mental slap on the wrist. Be nice, he told himself.

He parked carefully, locked the car, and walked into the restaurant behind Joyce trying to look relaxed.

A man in a very dapper sports coat and mock turtleneck sweater was standing by the little bar in sight of the entranceway. He set down his drink and walked briskly toward them.

"Ah, Mrs. Hill, Mr. Hill," he called out in a pleasant baritone voice. "You are very precise in your timing. I have just been speaking with the owner, Aldo. Aldo and I come from the same town in Italy."

Let me guess, thought Carl. Would that town be in the south? Perhaps on an island?

He took Carl's hand in a firm and warm handshake and Carl said how nice it was to meet in person.

"Please," Mr. Rizzo continued. "Our table has been prepared and Aldo has promised us a very special risotto."

As they approached their table, one of the waiters stood by ready to assist them to settle in. Mr. Rizzo ushered Joyce to the seat in the corner while he and Carl took chairs to either side of her facing each other.

"I admire your car," Carl offered.

"Thank you. It is a lot of fun to drive. Do you know sports cars?"

"A friend of ours has a '58 MGA," Carl responded. "I've helped him work on it. Well, mostly I hand him tools when he tells me what he needs. But we've done some road trips together with a car club. I really like the older British models like his and yours. Yours is a '59, isn't it?"

"Yes, and almost stock," Mr. Rizzo beamed. "I do most of the mechanical things myself. I worked as a mechanic for a while when I was a young man. That car is six years younger than I am. I'd like to have one from '53 to match the year of my birth, but the Healey from '59 is a much superior car."

They traded car stories for a few minutes until Mr. Rizzo, noticing that Joyce was being left out, changed the subject.

"I asked Aldo what he recommended for this evening," he said opening the menu but not looking at it. "He strongly suggested a primo of risotto made with some excellent scallops he has received this morning and either the osso buco or the lamb chops for the secondo. I have taken the liberty of choosing wines which will complement either."

"That sounds wonderful," said Joyce.

Carl made appreciative and agreeable noises and they settled on the risotto for everyone and the osso buco for Mr. Rizzo and Carl while Joyce chose to have the lamb chops as her main dish.

A waiter arrived with a basket of bread sticks, obviously handmade, and some very thin bread which broke off easily in your hand and was spiced with caraway. Water, both still and sparkling, appeared on the table while Mr. Rizzo instructed the waiter in Italian.

A white Gavi di Gavi and a red Dolcetto d'Alba made by Vietti arrived with six large Riedel glasses. Mr. Rizzo approved both wines and then turned toward Carl.

"I do apologize for intruding on your own business to ask your advice about my own," he said. "And I don't want to talk business over dinner. But, would you permit me to pose one question to you?"

"Of course, sir," Carl answered.

"I will, of course bring in some of my own people to get their opinion about the feasibility of the structural requirement of the project," he explained. "I would just ask you if, in your opinion, the location and local attractions would support such a business."

"I'm not an expert in the hospitality business," Carl said. "And this would, I think, have to be upscale to attract the right clientele. But I do think so," Carl told him honestly. "Of course, it would depend upon cost and financing."

"Excellent! Let us enjoy our meal then," Rizzo concluded.

The meal was excellent. Mr. Rizzo was a charming host and the restaurant clearly held him in esteem.

None of them drank very much, but the half empty bottles of Gavi and Dolcetto were swept away to be replaced by a 1995 single vineyard Barbaresco from Produttori del Barbaresco and a Barolo of the same vintage from Aldo Conterno. Carl knew both wines from visits to northern Italy, and knew also how expensive they would be in a restaurant here in Canada.

True to his word, Mr. Rizzo never raised a business topic for the rest of the meal.

As they sat back from the table after a dainty, but superb pastry accompanied by a glass of Moscato d'Asti from Saracco, Mr. Rizzo addressed Joyce.

"If you are willing to show us the property again on Friday, I will come back with one of my engineers. I'd like to ensure that the quarry can be modified to meet our needs."

Joyce, who had been quietly enjoying the meal and the discussion of various light subjects, focused her attention. "Certainly you can visit the property as you like. I can come with you or just give you the keys and let you look around all you want."

"That would be excellent," Mr. Rizzo told her. "I will confirm a time with you tomorrow and will come with my engineer then. We can look at the property ourselves. That way we will not take up any of your time."

As they drove home, Carl had to admit that Mr. Rizzo was exactly the opposite of what he had imagined. Sometimes even I'm too suspicious, he thought.

Chapter 30

A Face Card

**One of the three major cards containing caricatures:
Jack, Queen, King. The Jack is also known as the Knave.**

The drive to Detroit was a bit like taking a holiday, Carl thought. He had spent almost every minute of his life in New York before his recent move to Elmira. He'd never been outside the U.S.A. The only time he'd flown was when he was 19. He went to Florida with one of his friends, Roberto. They'd shared a number of minor robberies and they had delivered a stolen car one time to a warehouse in Jersey.

Roberto was delivering a package to someone in Miami for his father and Carl had been asked to go along as a paid guest. Carl had never known what was in the package and had never wanted to. It may have been money; it may even have been a simple gift.

Carl had assumed that he had been asked to go along just to make a more likely travelling pair. Or perhaps Roberto had suggested it to have a friend to share time in Florida with. Whatever the reason, Carl had enjoyed the trip. They arrived, checked into a beach front hotel, took a taxi the next day to a storefront operation and delivered the package into the hands of some guy he'd never seen before or since.

They had a week to themselves in Miami before flying home. The experience made Carl realize there was more to the world than New York. Before that trip, he'd never thought of travelling. After that trip he started looking at maps and imagining far away places. Someday he would travel, he'd thought.

On the drive to Detroit, Carl had realized that there was nothing holding him to one place now. He had called Stan from an airport to create the impression that he had gone somewhere far away. In the future that might be so. If this hit works out (for example, if he was not killed) and other work was sent his way in the future, he could live wherever he wanted.

In fact, he thought, it would be better to be out of sight. He had left New York, now he could find a quiet place to spend his life between hits. Elmira was perhaps too quiet. He would like to be near a university or college where he could take courses. School in the 'hood had been a place to meet people; no one he knew had ever actually studied. Now he had begun to see that there were things he could pick up that could be useful.

He planned to call Stan from the Detroit airport. He wanted again to give the impression of having flown in. He parked in short-term parking and walked into the arrivals area. He wasn't sure if the background noise from arrivals would sound different for the departure area, but it might.

He made the call to Stan and got confirmation that he was to go ahead. They had decided on the code "I'm hoping to get to see 'John' while I'm in town" to which Stan would respond something positive such as "Say hi for me," or "Have a nice time while you're there" to confirm that the hit was on, or something clearly negative such as "I don't think he's in town this week" to call it off.

Everyone enjoys playing at espionage, he thought. We're just big kids all our lives.

As he turned away from the bank of phones and headed back toward the parking lot, he saw a face in the crowd that was familiar.

It was Ronnie MacKenzie, a goofy sort of guy who ran errands for Stan and other people. Carl had never spoken to him and had never been involved in anything with him. Ronnie was four or five years older than Carl and of no interest to him. But, they each knew who the other was. Ronnie probably even knew that Carl (Wolf) had been spending time meeting with Stan in the last few months.

Their eyes met and there was recognition. Carl let his eyes slip away, passed Ronnie and hurried on his way. He almost expected to hear "Wolf! Fancy meeting you. What are you doing in Detroit?" or some similar expression of surprise. But there was nothing said and Carl was happy to get away without explanation.

In fact, Carl wondered what Ronnie was doing in Detroit. He wasn't important enough to be meeting anyone of significance, or even to be sent as a messenger.

For a moment his hyperactive defense instincts caused him to wonder if Stan was checking up on him. But Stan had no way of knowing when Carl would arrive in the Detroit area or to even expect him to be flying. It had to be pure coincidence, however unwelcome.

Carl drove to a downtown hotel fairly near the address he had for the bar run by the target. He corrected himself: "John". It was not wise to fall into the habit of using words such as target. You start thinking like that and the next thing you know, it pops out.

While still a young boy, his mother had told him he should respect people of all races and never use or even think pejoratives. Mom used words like that, words out of books. She didn't go very far in school, but she had enjoyed school and had continued to read widely. She was always bringing home books left at the hotel by departing guests, so she was used to reading all sorts of books. She encouraged Carl and he read far more than his friends, he guessed, although he never mentioned books to any of them.

The habit of reading and the thirst to understand things was a precious gift she had left to Carl. He often remembered that with gratitude. It was probably reading that had suggested some of the options he was now considering.

Books don't kill people; reading books kills people, he amused himself by thinking.

Too bad he could never share some of these jokes. He could only amuse himself by imagining the response they would evoke.

He picked up some take-out food from a nearby diner and ate in his room while going over the documents he had received by mail from Stan. There was nothing sinister in the file. It looked like the kind of notes one might have as an outline for a resume, including a couple of photos of "John." Still, under the heading of taking no chances, Carl would destroy them right after the job.

He made plans to walk to the neighbourhood of "John's" bar tomorrow. He would not enter the bar, except perhaps if he decided that the job could be done there. He wanted to check out the information he had received about "John" himself.

As was to become a habit with him, he cleaned and checked over his gun. He was using the same cheap .38 caliber which he had used in New York. If he survived this assignment he would never use it again. He would find a safe way to equip himself with a better gun, or guns, and establish a professional approach to this line of work.

He knew that he had a lot to learn. He intended to.

He watched a bit of a movie on T.V. and went to sleep easily as he always did.

Chapter 31

A Pair of Bullets

Two Aces in a hand, or even just turned up, are called "Bullets." Four Aces are referred to as "Full Metal Jacket."

Carl sat in the restaurant and looked at the bar across the street. He knew "John" was in there alone. He knew that the normal pattern was for the first of his employees to arrive at about 11:00. "John" didn't want to pay people for time when they weren't working, but he liked to check the cash and levels of liquor before the business started and at the end.

Tomorrow would be the day he would act.

He was tense; maybe he was even a lot tense. But he had his plan and he needed to just calmly walk through it.

When he had killed someone back in New York, his first official hit, it had been a drunken thug who could have been rolled by any tough guy wandering by.

This was a serious contractual take out of a well-established and presumably careful Wise Guy. Carl admitted to himself that he was nervous. Keep that feeling, he thought. Stay sharp and alert. Just don't let it get in the way of acting.

He had been in Detroit eight days. He had determined that "John's" pattern was predictable. He took to heart the warning that predictability can make one vulnerable.

"John" arrived at 10:00 every day. He stayed at the bar until it was open and serving drinks. Sometimes he stayed to eat lunch, sometimes he went off to do something and came back to oversee the supper hour. He was always at the bar from 11:30 at night until closing. He left by the back door about 30 minutes after his last employee and drove home in the car he kept parked right behind the back door.

Carl had ruled out hitting "John" at home.

Carl also ruled out hitting "John" after the bar closed.

He reasoned that if there was any time "John" would be nervous about being attacked it would be when he left the bar at night. He might even come out the back door with a gun in his pocket. He pictured the headline, Stupid gunman shot behind bar by owner.

The obvious problem of hitting him at the start of the day would be that the body would be discovered early. Was that a problem? It wasn't a problem for Carl. He wasn't expecting the cops to shut down the highways over the death of a guy like "John." Besides, he wasn't planning to go anywhere right away.

A shot or two at that time of day was also least likely to be heard or noted.

Just before 10:00 the ninth day since his arrival in Detroit, Carl was standing at the magazine rack in a store from which he could see the end of the alley where "John" drove in each morning.

When he saw "John" turn into the alley, he paid for a copy of an outdoors magazine and walked across to the end of the alley.

"John" was unlocking the back door as Carl walked past the end of the alley. He walked on for a few steps, put his hand to his forehead like someone remembering something and turned back and down the alley.

"John" was already inside. The door would be unlocked awaiting the arrival of the barkeeper.

Carl walked briskly down the alley, a man going somewhere. If someone else turned down the alley or was visible, he would keep walking and come out the far end of the alley which was in the direction of his hotel.

No one was visible, no one turned into the alley. When he reached the bar door, he casually opened it and walked in.

He had found out that the bartender's name was Pete.

"Pete! Are you here, Pete?" he called out from the doorway, having first closed the door behind him and taken out his gun. He stood with the gun held behind him as if he still had one hand on the doorknob. The magazine was non-threateningly on display in his other hand.

As he expected "John" came out of his office looking annoyed. "Pete won't be here for another hour. Who are you?"

"I brought him his keys," Carl responded, ignoring the question.

As Carl said this he shot "John" mid-body and stepped forward as he went down. He fired the second shot into the centre of "John's" head. He was definitely dead.

The .38 made one hell of a noise. This was the last time Carl would use a large caliber for his main gun.

Carl slipped the gun back in his pocket, walked out the back door and turned left to walk out to the far end of the alley. He never looked back. He walked at the same pace he had walked into the alley a minute earlier.

Carl went into a corner store two blocks away and bought a couple bottles of cola, a big bag of pretzels and a chocolate bar. He smiled to himself; might as well have a balanced lunch.

He shoved the magazine in the bag with his lunch provisions and walked casually back to his hotel, just an average guy doing some average shopping on an average day.

Back in his room, he sat in the overstuffed chair and turned on the television. Maybe there was a game of something on somewhere.

He decided that there was nothing he needed to do for at least twenty-two hours. He wouldn't worry that the police were going to kick down his door.

He started thinking what he would do tomorrow.

The structure he had put in place to be paid was simple. Stan would put the payment for the second hit in his bank account in New York which he had maintained. Then he would write a check on that account with his old signature making payment to his new name. It would work this time. But he needed a better system.

He wanted to have a route for the money that would be very difficult to connect to him. Now with some capital to work with, and the knowledge of corporate structures that he was acquiring, he would do that.

The second hit would net him $27,000 after about $3,000 in expenses. He now had a stake. He could set up a better system with more distance between himself and the hit.

He was uneasy about the fact that he had seen and been seen by Ronnie. Ronnie was one of the people who not only knew him from New York but also knew that he was connected to Stan. He was one of those who could surmise that Carl (Wolf) had taken out that small time thug in New York just before leaving town.

If Ronnie hadn't seen Carl (Wolf) he might have assumed, as no doubt many had, that Carl had been taken out himself. Now Ronnie knew he was still alive and Ronnie might even connect him with the hit in Detroit. Probably Carl was overestimating both his own significance and Ronnie's acumen. But it would have been so much better to never see anyone from the past again.

It was okay for Stan. Stan had status; he had connections and was protected. Stan's role as a distributor of contracts was common knowledge. It had to be known for people to make use of his service. No one would think of coming back on Stan for passing on a contract to hit someone. They would, on the other hand, be keen to revenge themselves of the shooter.

He decided that he wouldn't mention meeting Ronnie in Detroit. It would be interesting to see if word of it got back to Stan. Carl didn't intend to even contact anyone else in New York ever again. This would include his father. Despite having nothing against his father, Carl felt no bond and no reason to continue to know him.

Now he had realized that he didn't have to live in the U.S.A. to continue his activities. He considered moving to Mexico, but then took note of the advantages of living in Canada.

They spoke the same language that they did in the U.S.A., or near enough. They had a good health care system he'd heard, even if some Americans condemned it as being the spawn of godless communists. They opposed capital punishment and would not deport anyone to stand trial if the person faced the death penalty.

Actually the last factor didn't matter much to Carl. He had decided that he would rather be dead than in prison for a life term. He wasn't afraid of death; jail, being locked up, was one thing he just might admit he feared.

The other advantage of being Canadian, that is being a Canadian citizen if he could arrange that, was that they allowed dual citizenship. He could have his feet in two countries, or at least one foot in each.

Yet one more advantage was that from Canada he could vacation in Cuba. Ironically, before Castro a lot of the people he wanted to avoid used to go there a lot. Now Americans avoided Cuba.

Tomorrow he would check out of the hotel and drive back to Elmira. Maybe he would get rid of the gun and drive back through Canada.

Chapter 32

Cracking a new deck

At the beginning of a serious game, a fresh deck will be taken from an unopened package. If a card becomes bent, or marked in a way which might identify it from the back, a new deck will be introduced.

Carl bought a local paper the next day and read it over breakfast at the hotel. He had to search to find a mention of the 'Owner Shot at his Bar''. The short report mentioned that the bar was suspected of being an outlet for drugs.

After breakfast, he checked out and got his car out of the hotel parking area. He dropped a bag containing the newspaper wrapped around his handgun into a dumpster behind a restaurant. He drove carefully, obeying all street signs and lights to the border crossing.

He was surprised at the informality of his crossing into Canada at Detroit. The amount of traffic back and forth seemed to indicate that people regarded it as no different from traveling between Manhattan and Brooklyn.

He could easily have brought his gun with him since no one searched his belongings or asked much more than where he was born and where he was going. When he explained that he was

E. Craig McKay

driving through this section of Canada on his was back to the U.S. he was waved through and told to have a good day.

He had disposed of the gun because he never planned to use it again. He could afford to buy the gun that would work best for him. Also, he suspected that the gun probably had its own history with it. What a joke if he were arrested with it and charged for a crime he had not committed.

He had cleaned it well before dropping it into the dumpster. Occasionally guns are recovered from lakes and rivers; he doubted that the landfill sites were explored much once filled. Besides, the gun could not be traced to him. He had acquired it in a New York street in exchange for cash. He had not been asked for identification.

He saw some buildings offering to exchange currency and thought he had better do so. He soon found out that most restaurants and stores would accept U.S. dollars at about the same rate as offered in the exchange centres.

The few differences he discovered during his drive across to London, Hamilton, and St. Catharines assured him that he would have no difficulty adjusting to life in Canada if that indeed proved useful.

He decided to stop overnight in St. Catharines. His choice was based upon the fact that he was already near the border and he wanted to spend another day getting to know a bit of what Canada was like. Also, there were a number of motels right beside the highway which he could choose from.

He stopped at a Holiday Inn; no surprises was their motto, and indeed it was like any other Holiday Inn. He checked in at about 5:00 and decided to go to the bar to listen in on the conversations of locals. It could have been anywhere, he concluded. He discovered a drink he hadn't tasted before, a Bloody Caesar. It was basically a Bloody Mary with clamato juice (tomato juice mixed with clam juice, weird) in place of tomato.

The food offered in the restaurant was what he would expect at home too.

Breakfast had a few unusual items listed. He tried the full breakfast with peameal bacon and found it to his liking. He brought a local tourist brochure to the table and over his food and three cups of excellent coffee learned that there was a university and a college in the area and that Niagara-on-the-Lake was a historic town with a theatre festival.

Carl had a poor academic background, but his mother's passion for reading and the experience he was having taking some interest courses was opening up a taste for literature, business, and history.

He got a few directions from the front desk when he checked out and at their suggestion headed north through the city to the lake and then toward Niagara-on-the-Lake. He found the town attractive and very much enjoyed the drive beside the river. If he wanted to live in Canada and be near the border, this might be an area to consider.

He had never visited Niagara Falls, even though he had driven near there doing deliveries for the nursery; so, he parked his car there and behaved like the average tourist. He made a note to come back in summer to ride the Maid of the Mist.

His delivery job had finished at the end of August, so Carl had not had to ask for time off to go to Detroit. With the completion of this second job for Stan, he had enough to support himself without looking for work right away.

Carl wanted to establish himself with Stan, and had no firm idea how often a chance to do a job would be offered him. Stan had indicated that demand could vary considerably, but that he could count on at least two or three months between assignments. Carl liked that term, assignment, it sounded like something they gave out in school. It sounded a lot classier than going out to punch holes in someone's head.

Carl did a third hit in December. It felt a bit strange, what with the Christmas spirit and all, but it wasn't like the guy was Santa Claus. In fact, he was a loan shark, just as the Ebenezer Scrooge character had been.

The hit was in Chicago, so Carl was still able to drive in and out. This time, however, he rented a car. He had joined a gun club in Tonawanda. It was a bit far now, but it would be a good place to be a member if he moved to Canada. Belonging to a gun club meant he could buy virtually any gun he wanted, as long as it was not fully automatic. Of course the guns had to be registered in his name, but he didn't intend to leave one lying beside a body.

This hit went so smoothly it almost made him nervous. He scouted the area, observed the habits of "John", and after one trial walk by to confirm timing and sightlines, he popped the guy. He walked out the back door, got into his rental car and drove away. As far as he knew, no one ever found the body or reported the shooting. "John" might still be sitting in his office leaning back in his chair with two .22 slugs in the head.

Hit by the Dealer

When he drove home, he stayed stateside because he was carrying the gun and didn't want any hassle. He had a reasonable amount of money in the bank now and had his lawyer setting up two offshore corporations he could use later.

It was time for a bit of R & R, he figured. Maybe that trip to Cuba he'd imagined.

Using a tourist agent with connections in Canada, he booked a two-week all-inclusive at a hotel in Cayo Coco. She told him it was a new area of Cuba that was being opened up. The hotel name didn't mean anything to him, but it was five star and adult only, so he went along with her recommendation.

He had no one he wanted to be with over Christmas in the U.S., so he booked a period in Cuba which would span Christmas.

The flight from Toronto left on a Thursday morning six days before Christmas Day. Because he wanted to see a bit of a big city in Canada, he went over by bus a few days earlier. He checked into the Sutton Place in Toronto and spent two days walking and riding the trolley cars they called streetcars. He visited an art gallery and a museum. He discovered some restaurants and wandered through a large shopping mall that was crowded with Christmas shoppers.

The morning of December 19, he took a shuttle to the airport and boarded the flight to Cuba.

Carl was anxious to see what this bastion of communism would be like. Would they all wear grey uniforms like the Chinese Maoists?

When he arrived, he was a bit disappointed. It was warm, and the officials spoke Spanish instead of the English spoken in Canada, eh? But other than that it seemed normal.

The people from his plane were directed onto a bus. The bus stopped at a few other resorts on the way to his. They looked very nice from what he could see of them.

When they arrived at his hotel he was impressed by the grandeur of the arrival area. He could see through the open lobby into another open area with a pool. Looked pretty nice.

A driver with a golf cart took Carl and another couple to their buildings. His luggage would be delivered in a few minutes, he was told. Indeed, Carl had just finished exploring his second floor apartment with balcony facing the ocean, when there was a knock and his suitcase was brought in.

He had been asked to attend an orientation meeting near the main lobby at 5:00. It was just 4:30 so he changed into lighter clothing and walked back to attend it. The resort was filled with lush foliage which provided a sense of isolation. There were golf cart shuttles to move from one area of the resort to another, but the sinuous paved paths lined with tropical plants were a pleasure to stroll along. Carl didn't notice any insects which would have descended upon anyone walking outdoors on such a warm evening in the States.

He walked out of the meeting and headed toward the pool area he had noticed upon arrival. There was a long bar facing the pool with several people ordering drinks.

Carl walked up to the bar. Food and drinks were free here. Why, he wondered, did he have his wallet in his pocket?

He noticed one of the bartenders mixing exotic cocktails of some sort in a blender. People all seemed to be drinking pina coladas or mai tais. Carl ordered a beer from a bartender who looked over at him.

He noticed a woman near him who had been on his plane from Toronto. She looked as confused as he felt.

Her brown eyes were wide and made him think of a deer, or another soft, furry animal caught in a car's headlights.

"Is this your first time here too?" he asked her.

She turned to him and suddenly things shifted for him. Now he felt helpless and exposed.

He found himself telling her that it was his first time in Cuba. He told her that he was traveling alone. He told her that he was from the United States. He felt as if he would just keep talking and tell her everything about himself and then some things he didn't know.

Finally, he shut his mouth.

He felt like an idiot. Run, run, his instincts told him.

"I'm traveling with a friend from school," she told him. "We're here for two weeks. We'll miss the first few days of next term, but that's okay."

He excused himself as if he had somewhere to go.

She said "See ya."

He turned and lurched toward a path which seemed to go toward the beach. What a fool you are, he thought. Why did you speak to her? Why did you stop speaking to her? How are you going to avoid her for the next two weeks?

He found himself at the edge of a long, white beach. There was a beach bar in a hut nearby. He walked over to it and sat down at a table.

They had been told at the meeting that the main buffet dining room was open from 6:00 until 9:30. Carl looked at his watch and discovered that it was 5:45.

He wasn't hungry, but he decided that he would go to dinner early and spend the next two weeks hiding under his bed.

He returned to the main building and followed signage which indicated the dining room. It was huge and already bustling with diners. He picked up a plate from a stack and wandered toward one of the buffet tables. The table he came to had seafood and salads on beds of ice cubes.

He chose some things almost at random and turned to look for a place to sit.

"Hi there. Want to join us?" someone next to him asked.

He turned. It was her. Her eyes were still brown and he still felt foolish.

"Sure," he told her. What could he say? He had to get through this. He'd meet her friend. He'd chat with them. There would still be time to hide in his room after dinner.

She started to walk across the open area beside the buffet table, then turned and said "I'm sorry, I didn't introduce myself. I'm Joyce."

"I'm Carl," he said.

She led him to a small table near a window. There were two glasses with juice and two small plates with fruit. He suddenly realized that she was probably with her boyfriend who would be less welcoming to him than she had been.

"Here's Susan now," Joyce exclaimed and Carl turned to see another woman approaching.

"This is Carl," Joyce told Susan. "He came in on the same plane as we did."

"Oh," Susan responded. "Do you know this resort? It's our first time here."

"No, I've never been to Cuba before," Carl told her.

"We've been to another resort in Veradero," Joyce told him. "Our travel agent told us that the beaches here in Cayo Coco are the best."

They spoke of many things over dinner and Carl learned that the two women were starting their last semester at Brock University where they were in several classes together. Joyce was studying French with a minor in Spanish. Carl knew no French at all, but had picked up a bit of street Spanish growing up. He found that some of the bartenders understood him, but it wasn't a complicated topic.

Susan and Joyce both lived in St. Catharines. When he learned that they lived in the city he had considered as a base in Canada, Carl found plenty of questions to pose. He became so interested in all they had to tell him that he forgot to be ill at ease and found himself enjoying their company.

When he saw them by the pool the next day he went over and said hello. He wondered if they might not prefer to be by themselves, perhaps might be hoping to meet a couple guys traveling together.

Joyce was disarming in her open explanation of the relationship between the two women. Susan was married to a flight instructor from the St. Catharines airport. Because her husband was attending a training seminar over the Christmas period, Susan had invited Joyce to join her in Cuba. Susan's husband would be coming down to join them for the week after Christmas.

Carl told them that he was hoping to try scuba diving while in Cuba and asked if they had ever done that. Joyce had done an introductory dive the year before at the resort in Veradero, and said that she had brought a mask and snorkel with her this trip because she enjoyed swimming and exploring.

During the next week, Carl spent a lot of time on the beach and by the pool talking and swimming with Joyce and Susan. The more he learned about the Niagara Peninsula, as he learned it was called by locals, the more he thought it might be a good base for him.

Both women were bright and witty. He never felt like a third wheel and he found himself growing increasingly attracted to Joyce in many ways.

They went horseback riding together and discovered a common love of animals and respect for nature. The three of them went for a scuba session and spent many of the other days floating over the rock formations with snorkels, entranced by the sea life.

Carl also became aware of the problems the Cuban people faced because they had trouble getting things which Americans and Canadians took for granted, such as toothpaste, aspirins, even ball point pens. Susan and Joyce had brought a copious supply of these items with them and distributed them among hotel staff they met and people in the nearby town that they visited with organized groups.

He was impressed by the apparent lack of racial discrimination in Cuba. He learned of a Cuban aid society that existed in Canada. Volunteers gathered various items which could be reused in Cuba and through donation of free transport from airlines had them flown into Cuba to help the common people. Carl wished he had known these things before he came. He liked the idea.

Chapter 33

Queen of Hearts

In the Tarot deck, the Queen of Hearts is the Queen of Cups. In either deck, the card is associated with strong emotions and fulfillment.

By the time Susan's husband, Garth, joined them, Carl found that he and Joyce had become good friends.

The day before Garth arrived, Carl had a long talk with himself. The two women had gone off together on an organized trip to Havana. He had remained at poolside.

Carl had wanted to see Havana. However, he felt that he needed to get in touch with his feelings and work out where he was going.

Joyce was an interesting woman. He felt attracted to her. He felt that she liked him too and he even had the sense that it could develop into something serious. But he was concerned about several things.

Was a hit man a good choice for anyone to partner with? Could he work in the field he was just beginning without sharing the knowledge of what he was doing with someone he would be intimate with? Carl was fairly conservative about many things.

He believed in being honest in relationships and keeping his word.

The other major worry he had was that what they were sharing might just be a vacation romance. He was afraid that when they got back to their respective everyday lives they would find they had nothing in common.

When Garth arrived the next day, the four of them had supper together at one of the special restaurants at the resort. Garth was an interesting fellow and he and Carl seemed to hit it off well.

After dinner, Susan and Garth had clearly wanted to spend a little time alone, so he and Joyce walked down to the beach and along the sand.

They stopped to look at the moonlit sea and quite naturally embraced and kissed. They drew apart and he said the least romantic thing she might have expected. "We need to talk."

"You're married, aren't you?" Joyce asked.

"Me? No. Why? Are you?" Carl said, sensing that he might be heading back toward the babbling stage.

"No, I'm not," Joyce said. "It just seemed there must be something. It feels like you've been keeping me at arm's length. Susan thought so too."

My God, thought Carl. Women talk about everything. I've been a topic of discussion without realizing it.

"Is this better?" he asked drawing her toward him.

"It feels very nice," she purred.

"Good. It feels very nice to me too," he told her.

They separated gently and continued to walk across the smooth sand.

After a few minutes Joyce said, "What did you want to talk about then?"

Carl didn't tell her about his gun-for-hire activities, but he told her most other things about himself. He shared his feelings toward her and his hope that this could be more than a two week fling. He told her he had been considering moving to Canada and had even picked out St Catharines as a possible new home. He said he had nothing to keep him in the States.

Joyce also shared some details. She had come to Canada from England with her mother in 1974 when she was ten. Her birthday, June 24, was exactly 2 weeks later than Carl's.

Her father had died in an industrial accident and Joyce's mother had been offered a job with her sister-in-law's business in St. Catharines.

She asked him about what he would do in Canada and he told her that he had some money saved up and wanted to get some professional training and take some business courses.

After a while Joyce told him that she also hoped their mutual attraction would last when they were back up north. "We'll just have to wait and see," she added practically.

"Take it one day at a time and enjoy it while we can?" he questioned her.

"Something like that, yes," she replied.

Then, for what was not to be the last time, Joyce took him completely by surprise.

She leaned against him and he felt his whole body grow warm as she said "One day at a time sounds fine; one night at a time too. I'd like to sleep with you tonight."

During the rest of the vacation in Cuba, Carl learned a lot about Joyce, her history, her interests, her aspirations. He hoped that their feelings would survive the transition when they went back home.

He decided that all he could do was see what happened. He had heard it said that we need to live in the moment more. The moments he was living now were excellent.

Chapter 34

Being Rivered

The three times cards are laid face up for common use by the players are called: The Flop, when the first three cards are turned up; The Turn, when one more card is turned up; and The River, when the fifth common card is laid face up. To be beaten by another player on the basis of that final, or River card, is referred to as being rivered.

Just before leaving for the office Thursday, Joyce mentioned that she wanted to get her car serviced Friday. She asked Carl if he could drive in with her and drop her off at work.

"I can get a ride over to pick it up when it's ready," she said. "But I'd like to drop it off early and no one else from our direction is going into the office tomorrow morning."

"No problem at all," Carl told her. "I want to drive into St. Catharines to pick up some things for the boat. It's almost time to winterize her and I want to find out how much a mooring just up river from Niagara-on-the-Lake would cost. What would you think about us moving her down below the Falls next year?"

"That would be a great idea," Joyce responded warmly. "We talked about how nice it would be to visit the Thousand Islands."

"Good, I hoped you would think so. I'll see if there's a mooring available for next spring and how much they're asking."

Reflections was a vintage Chris Craft from 1972, which made her about eight years younger than either Joyce or Carl. He could hardly refer to her as "the old girl", but she was old enough that people often would come over when he pulled into a strange marina and want to talk about the similar boat they used to own.

She had been well maintained by the previous owner and Carl had updated the fuse box and electronics. His present VHF radio was new this year and was connected to a very good GPS. He didn't have radar, so he would avoid traveling on days which threatened fog, but he felt confident in her and his own ability to handle most navigation problems.

Although *Reflections* was only 26 feet in length, her nine and a half foot beam made her interior spacious for a small cabin cruiser. He had not wanted too large a boat, but he definitely wanted to have an onboard galley and head. The 350 hp inboard/outboard was a very reliable propulsion unit, and he was careful to inspect, and also to have inspected, all the mechanical aspects each season.

Joyce enjoyed boating with him, although she was often concerned that their present mooring put them on the wrong side of the Falls. Moving down river would increase their ability to enjoy the boat.

Now that he would not be on-call for Stan, Carl would be able to plan some holidays without fearing he might have to make a change at the last minute.

Chapter 35

A Joker in the Pack

Although new packs of cards come with one or two Jokers, those cards are removed from the deck before playing Texas Hold'em. To discover a Joker during play would be both surprising and disturbing.

Joyce parked her car at the Audi dealership and turned over a partial set of keys.

Carl turned around while waiting for her to come back out. He was especially careful not to back into a sporty TT convertible which he rather fancied. He would like to drive one of those through the Grosglockner Hockalpenstresse. He and Joyce had driven this high pass through the Alps when they combined a holiday at Zell am See in Austria with a visit to Torri del Benaco on Lago di Garda in Italy.

That was in September two years ago. Carl smiled inwardly as he remembered how they had met cattle, decorated with bells and flowers, being herded down from summer pastures to winter cow sheds.

You could drive for two days and still be in one province in Canada, whereas Joyce and he had been dining on very good

Austrian schnitzel beside an Austrian lake one evening and equally wonderful Italian pasta beside an Italian lake the next.

Joyce climbed in beside him and he shared his thoughts with her. They both smiled as they remembered how much fun they had on that trip.

"We should take that cruise we've been talking about," Carl said.

"Which one?" she teased. "We've been looking at so many."

"Let's take them all," he countered.

"All at once?"

"Well, we'll start with only one. How about that 11-day cruise from San Juan, Puerto Rico that we looked at for this November?" Carl suggested.

"I'm game if you are," Joyce told him. "November and December are usually slow months here in real estate. Are you able to go then?"

"I've decided to not let work get in the way of pleasure," Carl told her. "I'll check the prices and availability on line and we can talk about it tonight."

"Yes, please!"

They parked in front of the real estate agency and Carl got out to help Joyce carry some files into the office.

As he was opening the trunk to get them, a large black car pulled up behind his grey Mercedes. He turned casually and found himself staring at a face he recognized.

The chauffeur of the Lincoln Limousine was someone he had hoped to never see again, Ronnie MacKenzie. It was almost twenty-five years since he'd seen Ronnie at the Detroit airport, but he was sure this was him.

He forced his gaze to slide away. Ronnie was getting out of the car and may not have recognized Carl; surely he wouldn't after all these years. But he had recognized Ronnie.

Carl turned away as Ronnie crossed in front of the limo and headed toward its curbside rear door. Carl carried the files into the office and watched as Mr. Rizzo and a larger man got out of the limo. Ronnie closed the door behind them and went back to sit in the driver's seat.

Joyce was saying hello to Mr. Rizzo and being introduced to the other man. Carl watched from inside the front office and positioned himself to be out the sightline of Ronnie should he look over at the agency.

Joyce led Mr. Rizzo and his companion into the office. Carl greeted Mr. Rizzo and was introduced to his engineer. They had come to pick up the keys to the property.

"Do you mind if I use your phone to make a call?" Carl asked Joyce. "I've forgotten to bring my mobile and I'd like to confirm my appointment."

"Of course," Joyce said.

Carl excused himself and left Joyce and the two men to the business of obtaining keys.

Carl went to Joyce's desk in one of the rear cubicles and busied himself in making a totally pointless phone call to the marine supply company in St. Catharines to ensure they had some biodegradable antifreeze.

As he had hoped, the two men left with the keys a minute or so later and Joyce came back to join him at her desk.

"Everything okay?" she asked.

"Yep, I just wanted to check that they had what I need in stock before driving down there."

"Okay. Thanks for the ride. I'll be home this afternoon unless something else comes up," Joyce assured him. "Maybe we can look at the cruise details together."

"I'd like that," Carl said. "Looks as if Mr. Rizzo is serious."

"Yes, it does. Thanks to you for that great idea you had."

Yes, Carl thought. I'm full of great ideas.

As he drove toward St. Catharines, his mind raced. What if Ronnie did recognize him?

What would Ronnie do?

What would he do? He felt as if he'd been blindsided. He hadn't seen this coming.

If Ronnie was his personal chauffeur, there was every likelihood that Mr. Rizzo was not the innocent businessman he pretended.

Maybe the limo was part of a fleet. Ronnie could be working for someone not associated directly with Mr. Rizzo.

That doesn't matter, Carl reminded himself. It was whether Ronnie had recognized him.

If he had, would it matter?

Ronnie had been a fringe player a quarter of a century ago. Was it likely that he was connected now? Even if he was, so what? How would Ronnie know that Carl had been working freelance for Stan? Why would he care? What could he do? Why would he want to do anything?

Too many questions.

Carl drove into St Catharines and picked up some supplies he wanted for the boat. As he drove by a payphone he thought about calling Stan.

Chapter 36

Washing the cards

As part of shuffling the cards when a new deck is introduced, the dealer will often spread the cards out on the table and use both hands to move them about to mix and intermingle them.

As they flew back from Cuba, Toronto, and all of southern Ontario, was blanketed in snow; Lake Ontario lay grey and green, a dark and somber body of icy water. The cold air outside the terminal was a shock to them after even such a short time away from it. The four of them shared a shuttle from the Toronto airport back to St. Catharines where Susan and Garth were dropped off first at their apartment in north St. Catharines.

Joyce lived with her mother in a house in a nearby wartime housing subdivision. Joyce had arranged for Carl to stay over that night in their guest room and he would take a bus back to Elmira the next day.

Carl met Joyce's mother, Eileen Frost, and they had coffee and cake together while Joyce showed her mother brochures and souvenirs she had brought back from Cuba. Carl tried to pretend he didn't realize that he was being evaluated. He responded to questions about his family and employment history carefully, putting emphasis on the courses at Buffalo University that he was taking and his interest in business.

Although as Wolf he had not been an outstanding student in New York, he had managed to graduate from grade 12 with decent marks, and his penchant for reading meant that he was aware of a lot of things which most of his cohort would have been surprised to discover.

Carl knew that people like talking about themselves, so he steered the topics back to Eileen's past as often as he could. By doing so he learned that Joyce's father, Walter, had been born in Canada and had met her mother while working at Canada House in London 15 years after the end of WWII. He had died in a traffic accident in 1975, just after Joyce turned eleven.

Eileen had then moved to Canada to take a secretarial position in a company where her sister-in-law was a partner. They had lived with Aunt Ellen and her husband Clive for a year before Eileen was able to buy the small bungalow where they now lived.

Carl thought that Joyce's mother had her reservations about this strange young man from New York City, but she seemed willing to give him a chance. For his own part, he liked Eileen and hoped that she would come to like him. He hoped that at least she wouldn't actively discourage Joyce from seeing him.

He was very careful to avoid being too overtly familiar with Joyce that evening and to avoid touching her, although they had got to know each other pretty well in the past two weeks. They had slept side by side for the last six nights and he would miss that tonight when he was consigned to the guest room.

Carl, as was typical for him, slept well that night and was well rested when he came to the kitchen dining area in the morning to join Joyce and her mother for breakfast.

Joyce was going to the University for a class later that morning and dropped Carl off at the bus depot.

While he was waiting he asked about books and was directed to a used book store a couple blocks away. There he picked up a few books with information about the Niagara Region, an old business directory, and a couple novels. He bought the local newspaper, The St. Catharines Standard, and read through it on the bus ride back to the United States.

Less than an hour later he got off the bus in Buffalo and picked up his car.

He kept thinking about Joyce. Now more than ever he was interested in moving to St. Catharines.

Chapter 37

High Card

The weakest type of hand. The player hopes his highest card is higher than the other player(s) card(s).

Carl and Joyce saw each other two or three times per week during the next month. Carl would stay over on a night when he had a class in Buffalo or was participating in a shooting match in Tonawanda. He got on well with Joyce's mother and realized that she liked him too.

By the end of March, Carl was sure what he wanted. Joyce was a major part of his plans for the future and he was determined to do his best to get her to accept him. He gave two weeks notice to Mrs. Clark, explaining that he had a chance to go to school in Canada and would have to move there.

He found an apartment in St. Catharines, and sold his car at a very fair price to his school teacher fellow boarder, Carol. Carol was excited about having her first car, and Carl felt good knowing that the car was worth more than he charged her.

He would miss some aspects of Clark's boarding house, but he was looking forward to cooking for himself.

He purchased a good set of pots and pans and cooking utensils. Carl appreciated the importance of using good quality instruments. It is said that a tradesman should not blame his tools, but it is easier to do good work with good tools than inferior grade ones.

A set of Henkel knives was kept well honed and within easy reach of his food preparation area and he had several good quality cutting boards. One item which might have seemed out of place was a large cast-iron frying pan. The even steady heat which the well- seasoned pan provided was useful for many dishes including the caramelizing of onions or toasting slivered almonds for salads. Carl also used it to prepare the various styles of curry he enjoyed making. He even bought a marble pizza stone which could also be used to make Indian flat breads to go with the curry.

It became a source of pleasure to prepare meals for Joyce. He even invited Susan and Garth to dinner a couple of evenings. All four of them enjoyed conversation over a meal.

Though Garth had a strict rule that he never drank alcohol within 12 hours of flying and none of them overindulged, they often enjoyed trying a new wine with food.

The Canadian winemakers had turned the page on the mediocre wine of their early years and were now producing wines of complexity and character. It became a bit of a game for the four of them to discover an interesting wine, either domestic or imported, which they could pair with a specific meal.

Carl's first experience with wine had been as a child when sharing a meal with one of his childhood friends. Many of their parents were immigrants who had brought with them the practice of enjoying wine with meals and even giving small glasses of watered wine, or wine with ginger ale added, to children of ten or more. Carl had noticed that the children of such families seldom became binge drinkers in the way that many others did. The idea that there be a specific age before which one could not drink at all and then suddenly one day there was no limit made no sense to him.

While living in Elmira, Carl had visited some of the wineries of the Finger Lakes and enjoyed discovering the protocol of serious wine tasting. When he moved to Canada he started visiting the wineries there and well remembered the pleasant discovery of a Chardonnay produced by Cave Springs.

Wine makers were always ready to talk with anyone who showed an interest. When visiting Inniskillen one time, Carl met Don Ziraldo and also vintner Karl Keiser who was very keen on attempting to grow Pinot Noir in the Niagara Region. Karl had charts and graphs which showed the similarity in latitude and sun hours between their vineyards and those of Burgundy, the most famous producers of Pinot Noir.

Carl wasn't a fan of the red wines being produced in Canada during the 1980s but he enjoyed many of the white wines. He also loved driving along the Niagara Parkway where Don Ziraldo had a home. Carl little guessed then that he and Joyce would live nearby fifteen years later.

He and Joyce had dinner together at his apartment at least three times a week and she often stayed over. Carl sensed that she felt as comfortable with him as he did with her.

He had no clear idea where his life would take him. Perhaps he would end up face down in a gutter somewhere. He believed that he could put it all together, but it was possible that he was just an accident waiting to happen.

Carl was not a fatalist. He believed that we make our own future. He believed in himself. Win or lose, he would get the credit or the blame.

Chapter 38

A Pair

Two cards of the same value: two 2's weakest, two aces strongest.

Through his competitive shooting of hand guns at the Tonawanda Gun Club, Carl had met some shooters from Canada. He asked one of them about shooting clubs in the St. Catharines area and was invited to join Pine Hill Gun Club.

Their clubhouse shooting range was quite small, but he was given a key and could use it whenever it was convenient. By joining their competition team, he was able to get a permit which allowed him to cross the border with a gun.

In theory, the permit was only valid to go to and from matches, but since there were literally hundreds of matches going on every day somewhere in the U.S., that posed no actual limitation.

Since he could not expect to drive to all locations where his services might be needed and he didn't want his presence there noted, Carl had to solve two concerns. How could he take a gun, or guns with him if he needed to travel on an aircraft and how could he avoid his name turning up in those locations he visited.

Carl knew that computer searches could be devised that would sift though huge data banks looking for common aspects. Carl did not intend to be a common factor tying two or three similar executions together.

The acquisition of guns in the U.S. was not difficult. Therefore, he decided that he would purchase guns as needed and rent storage for them near wherever he bought them where they could be picked up if he needed them again. It would be best if neither the guns nor the storage lockers could be connected with him. As long as the storage lockers or safety deposit boxes were in some other name, Carl could just walk away from them if he needed to.

That brought him back to the second concern: concealing his own name. What I need is a secret identity, he realized. Just like a super hero. I could call myself "Hitman" and wear a costume, or better yet become a brand new caped crusader. Turning serious, he began considering what he needed.

Unless he was planning to use the identity for international travel, all he really needed was a driver's license and a credit card. Could he obtain those? He thought he could. He did, after all, have some criminal connections.

Stan was more than just another pretty face. He was able to put Carl in touch with someone who was what might be called a resurrectionist. This contact found dead people who could be brought back into the main stream. It was a sort of reincarnation.

The concept of a free market system is that if a need exists someone will find a way to meet that need in return for money.

Carl was not the first person to want a second identity. His contact was in the business of supplying them.

The process was fairly simple. Research into burial records and death certificates yielded up a plenteous supply of persons who, through the natural process of mortality, ceased to have need of worldly things such as birth certificates and social insurance numbers. One such identity was found and supplied to Carl.

The individual, Calvin Bridges, had been born a year after Carl and had died tragically at the age of four. His social insurance number had, as occasionally happens, not been cancelled. It was possible for Carl to assume the number and name as a secret identity.

He then, as Calvin Bridges, rented an apartment for a few months, opened a bank account in Buffalo using that address, signed up for a credit card at the bank, obtained a driver's license, used the credit rating he established over the next year to obtain a second credit card and had everything he needed to travel unnoticed. Guns he needed for professional use were purchased using the name Bridges. Although he didn't need it yet, he could even get a passport issued in that name.

Carl obtained all the permits required for his participation with Pine Hill competition shooting. He registered all those guns properly and was fastidious in obeying the laws regarding storage and transporting them. He was a model gun collector and club member. Carl was not interested in hunting or fishing, although he loved being in the wilderness and thought about getting a small boat.

Chapter 39

Two Pair

Any two pair will beat any single pair. If both players have two pairs, the hand with the highest wins; e.g., Ace-Ace and 2-2, beats King-King and Queen-Queen.

Because of Joyce's major in French, she was interested in possibly traveling to France. Carl wanted to share her interests, and he also thought it would be a good idea to find out more about international business possibilities.

He contacted Brock University and inquired about the possibility of taking courses. There were some restrictions on credit courses, but he could take non-credit courses that interested him and they showed him how he could upgrade his academic qualifications to be admitted as a part-time student.

One of the first courses he signed up for was a conversational French course and he found that he had some aptitude for languages. Joyce helped him and he found he enjoyed the idea of being able to speak another language. He had noticed that in Canada people seemed to value multilingualism.

Soon he and Joyce found themselves discussing the possibility of going to France in the summer. Carl did some research and before he knew it they were booked for a flight to Paris for early July of 1986.

As a special surprise and treat for Joyce and himself, Carl reserved a table for lunch at the Michelin Star restaurant *Jules Verne* in the Eiffel Tower. It was an unusual extravagance for Carl, but he was earning good money, and what was the point if he couldn't splurge once in a while. He was also aware that, careful as he tried to be, he could be killed if he made a mistake. That's why I get the big money, he remembered.

He had just finished reading some poetry of Edna St Vincent Milay which seemed to apply. Specifically her poems about living for the moment seemed appropriate:

> *Safe upon the solid rock the ugly houses stand.*
> *Come and see my shining palace built upon the sand.*

Carl knew he was living on the knife's edge. Life was for the living.

Chapter 40

Three of a Kind

Enough to get into trouble. It beats many hands but loses to many also. Three of a kind is also referred to as 'a set'.

Stan contacted Carl in May of 1986 with an offer of a contract hit in Altoona, Pennsylvania.

Carl was keen to become a regular with Stan, so he accepted the contract although it looked from the documents he was sent that this might be a tricky job. The "John" was a major player in the drug and prostitution rings in the region and had lots of connections.

It was this hit that almost got Carl killed.

The best part about Altoona was that Carl didn't have far to drive. Since he had never traveled much he decided to take the scenic route. This took him through such major centers as Troy, Alba, Canton, Roaring Branch, and Trout Run before hitting Williamsport. The next day he drove to Lock Haven before cutting down to join the 220 which he followed into Altoona.

The upcoming job was on his mind and he was happy to settle into a Holiday Inn. No surprises, please. He got a map and located "John's" major hang out in a seedy area of Pleasant Valley Blvd.

With his New York plates he felt as if he stood out. He made a mental note to consider a local rental car for future assignments. Carl wasn't visiting as a tourist, but he couldn't help noticing the attention paid to railroading in Altoona. There were museums to trains and thematic shops all over. Well stay on track yourself, he mused.

"John" tended to be active late in the day and into the later hours. So Carl looked around town a little in the mornings.

He spent a week getting to know the area and thought he had a good sense of "John's" habits and timetable. He was wrong. It was because of this experience that Carl started carrying a back up gun with some take-out power. It was also a lesson to take his time and be sure.

Carl had decided to take out "John" as he got out of his car at a strip joint he visited on business every night.

There was a parking place "John" always used near the back door. The manager of the club parked another vehicle in the spot and when "John" arrived, "John" honked his horn three times and the manager, or someone else, came out and moved that car to the front of the building.

Carl had worked out that when the manager drove toward the front of the club and "John" pulled into the then vacant spot, there would be an opportunity. He had watched "John" park here on six previous nights. "John" was always alone.

The night he decided to make his move, Carl arrived before "John" was due and was waiting when he pulled in and honked his horn. The manager came out, waved at "John," got in his car and drove away.

There was no one else in the parking lot. There were no windows at the back of the building. This was it.

As soon as "John" pulled into the spot and turned off the engine, Carl was out and walking toward the car from behind. He had his .22 revolver held down by his side.

The .22 Carl carried was a special gun. It was a revolver, so it didn't leave shell casings behind and couldn't jam easily. With a semi-automatic, the recoil cycles the slide action. If the bullet is a dud, the recoil isn't enough and the slide must be cycled by hand to eject the dud and load the next round. Occasionally the dud may even have to be pried out with your fingers before the gun will cycle.

Also, the Smith & Wesson 617 .22 had a cylinder which held seven rounds instead of six. Smith and Wesson also made a five shot revolver of .45 calibre, but that was of less interest. Carl had his eye out for a compact .38 to fill the role of back-up.

Because he was using a .22 he wanted to be very close to "John" when he shot him. The bullet had to penetrate the skull on the way in. Once it was inside the skull it could ricochet around a bit. No exit wound, no mess.

"John" was a slow moving man. He was still getting out of the car as Carl came up behind him.

"John" never saw him. Carl raised the gun, placed it close to "John's" head just behind the left ear, and pulled the trigger twice.

That was when the big guy got out of the other side of the car.

Carl saw the other man reach into his coat. As if in slow motion the hand came back out holding a very big gun.

The hours of practice at the range helped Carl now. Just as if he were on the firing line as the targets turned, Carl brought his little .22 on target and put three shots in a tight group in the big guy's forehead.

Carl was expecting the guy to shoot back. Then, as if he were just sitting down, the gunman crumpled down on the other side of the car. Carl turned on his heel, walked to his car, got in, and drove away.

That was it. It was over. But Carl decided that he had better have a serious talk with himself when he got a chance. Don't assume the target is alone: look. He also promised himself that he would get a suitable back up gun before the next job. With a . 38 in his left hand he could have shot the guy through the open car doors.

In poker, two hands which tie in other aspects are decided by the extra card or cards. The extra card is known as a kicker. The same name is applied to an auxiliary motor on a boat. It could equally be used to describe a back up gun, thought Carl. Kicker is very important.

There was another lesson to remember. A gun is only good once it's in your hand. He was only able to shoot first because his gun was out while the big guy was still reaching for his.

Chapter 41

Straight

A series of five cards. Ace can be top in 10, J, Q, K, Ace or bottom in Ace, 2, 3, 4, 5. Fairly strong since it beats everything up to three of a kind.

Joyce and Carl arrived in France in July with plans of visiting everything. Before long they realized that although Europe looks small on a map compared to North America, there were so many places to visit and things to see that it was better to spend less time driving and more time in each place.

During that visit the summer of 1986, they spent one week in Paris and two weeks driving down the Rhone Valley as far as Avignon and back up to Paris. It was on that trip that they learned of the summer drama festival at Avignon and made plans to go back there the next year.

They visited the obvious tourist locations in and near Paris, the Louvre Museum, Napoleon's Tomb, the roof of the Arch de Triumph, Fontainebleau, Versailles, and the tower Eiffel had built for the World Fair.

As with everything he did, Carl researched the trip ahead of time and made plans. For example, the 1400 some fountains at Versailles are not left running all the time. It is only on weekends during the spring and summer that they are turned on and accompanied by live music. This is called *Grandes Eaux Musicales*, or Fountain Shows. They went to Versailles twice, once to view the palace and again on a weekend to visit the fountains. It was magical. Joyce loved it and at this point Carl knew that he loved her.

The lunch at the Jules Verne was expensive, but very good. The experience of eating in the tower was one they would never repeat, and would never forget. In order to make it happen, Carl had reserved a table two months earlier.

When he and Joyce arrived at the red-carpeted walkway at the foot of the tower, they walked in behind another couple of Americans. Once all four of them were inside the foyer, the couple in front were asked if they had a reservation. When they admitted that they had not reserved, they were informed that the restaurant was *complet*, full. The man attempted to offer a monetary inducement, but was firmly informed that it was not possible.

Since Joyce and Carl had reservations, they were ushered into the Jules Verne private elevator and carried up to the restaurant floor. Already the experience felt special. When seated, they discovered that there were indeed empty tables but that the restaurant only allowed half the tables to be used at lunch to provide a better experience for their customers. This was a real eye opener for Carl. In North America, restaurants habitually fill every table possible and even have more than one seating to maximize profit. Imagine a restaurant putting quality of the client's experience before cash flow.

After the week in Paris, they drove south using the Michelin Red Guide to find inexpensive but comfortable places to stay and good meals. They loved driving the national roads which were lined with plane trees and led through the narrow central streets of towns. They both tried everything offered to them and found most things much to their liking.

In Beaujolais they visited each of the ten special communes with are called the cru Beaujolais. They tasted the various cru and each picked favorites. Carl liked best Morgon and Regnie while Joyce favored Moulin a Vent and St Amour.

As they moved farther south they experienced the variety of ways duck can be prepared and enjoyed the wine of the Rhone valley with many styles which went far beyond the standard Canard a l'Orange served in many North American restaurants.

Many of the villages in the wine regions were having celebrations while they were there, so they altered their plans as needed to participate in many of them. They stayed overnight in Chateauneuf de Pape, L'Isle-sur-la-Sorgue, and Avignon.

The three weeks were crowded with adventure and excitement. They seemed too soon over, and they both talked about returning to see more.

This trip with Joyce was an important step in their relationship. Traveling together for three weeks, sleeping together, eating together, making decisions together, is a good way to find out if you get along. They did.

There was another indicator which Carl made a note of. Carl had noticed on trips with other people that a certain tension often happened at the end of a trip. It was as if people, having been forced to be together for a period of time, were eager to have their freedom back. This didn't happen when he and Joyce got back to Canada.

They went to their separate homes that first night home, but they were very comfortable with each other the next morning and spent the day recalling things they had seen and making plans for future trips together.

Chapter 42

Flush

Five cards all of the same suit (e.g., spades). The highest card, or cards, determine which flush is highest.

That September, Carl enrolled part-time at Brock. Joyce had decided to spend one more year to turn her degree into a double major, so they spent a lot of time at the university together.

His love of reading led Carl to register in literature courses and he soon found himself considering applying for admission to a degree program. He didn't imagine that Stan, or any of the people who Stan subcontracted him for, would want to view his Curriculum Vita, but Carl liked structure and it was pleasant to have a goal.

They also went out with Susan and Garth fairly often. Once, Garth asked Carl if he'd like to go for a ride with him. Garth often was asked to deliver a plane for someone. Carl had responded enthusiastically; he'd never been up in a small plane.

He found Garth a very interesting person. Garth was serious and dedicated to his job as a flight instructor. If he was typical of the kind of person who became an airline pilot, passengers were in good hands. Garth checked weather conditions even on days when most people would say there was no chance of bad weather conditions. He always used a printed checklist and insisted that his students inspect the plane visually themselves rather than just taking his word for it that all was correct.

Garth would have made a good hit man, but he didn't like guns. Carl invited him to come to the club, but Garth said that although he knew that target shooting was just like a dart competition, he preferred darts.

Chapter 43

Full House

A set (3 of a kind) and a pair in one five card hand beats a flush. It is also referred to as 'a tight', or 'being tight'.

Garth contacted Carl in early October with an offer to go with him to Centre Island, Toronto. They were just going to fly a small plane over there and then get a ride back with another pilot.

They left St. Catharines at about 9:00 one Tuesday morning. Garth was pleased to explain the kind of preparation that every pilot should go through when making even a short flight to a familiar airport.

Carl found it fascinating. Like many others probably, he had assumed that the hard part of flying was the actual steering and maneuvering of the plane. He was surprised to learn that trip planning, checking weather, map reading, navigation and radio procedures were at least as significant.

Garth explained how major centres like Toronto, which had several traffic control areas overlapping and both IFR and VFR air traffic, required a pilot to understand in advance how to handle the radio protocol to ensure a safe and appropriate entering and proceeding through the zones and areas.

They were going to the Toronto Island Airport, but couldn't fly straight across Lake Ontario because they were crossing water and would have to remain within gliding distance to shore for safety reasons. They couldn't just fly really high because that would put them in conflict with the Toronto International Airport control area.

They would have to leave the St. Catharines control zone heading west, go along the shoreline while climbing to about 6,000 feet. Then they could head north toward the other shore and turn east. That, however, would take them into a 25 mile zone controlled by Toronto. They would have to follow radio given directions about course and altitude as they proceeded easterly and as they neared the 5 mile control zone of the Island Airport, they would need to obtain permission to enter and land.

When Carl saw the attention to detail involved in preflight and flight checks as well as the complicated protocol involved in just moving along taxiways, he gained a new respect for the aviation profession.

He also resolved to apply some of the planning and check list procedures to his own trade.

Chapter 44

Four of a Kind

Four cards of the same value (e.g., four 7's). Highest are best.

One clear day in the autumn, Garth took Carl and Joyce up to see the Niagara River and the Falls from the air. They had gone together on the Maid of the Mist and experienced the immense power of the thundering cascade of water. Now, as they circled above the mist, the mighty Niagara seemed but a ribbon of green and white froth.

Perspective is everything, thought Carl. To most people his contractual engagements to kill people would seem savage as well as criminal. But how did it really differ from the mercenaries, or soldiers, who signed up to kill on command? Yes, we are told that some wars are fought for noble goals, but are both sides fighting for noble goals? Surely at least one side must be wrong; and if one side is wrong, perhaps both sides are.

Perhaps I am no saint, Carl thought, but if I ever think that the person I am hired to shoot is a good person, at least I can choose not to shoot.

That caused Carl to resolve to refuse any contract which he would personally consider wrong. I will not act against my own convictions, he decided. I will not fall back on the old excuse that I am just following orders. If what I do is wrong, it is my wrong doing. I will not be a thoughtless instrument.

Maybe I should take some Philosophy courses, he thought, and laughed at his own pomposity.

Instead he took some English literature courses and conversational French. His source of income left him lots of time for reading, even when on location and he wanted to share something in which Joyce was interested. People who don't grow together grow apart, he believed.

Chapter 45

Straight Flush

A straight made up of cards which are also of the same suit.

While in the air over the river they had noticed a few boats on the water, even now with summer well over. Joyce pointed out a cruiser working its way up river against the strong current. It was just below the Queenston-Lewiston bridge and seemed to be bound for the dock at the Riverside restaurant they had dined at one sunny Saturday.

Carl asked Joyce if she liked being in a boat on the water and was pleased to learn that she had sailed several times with her aunt on a northern lake where her Aunt Ellen and Uncle Clive had a waterfront cottage.

Joyce told him that the small family group of her mother, Ellen, Clive, and Clive's brother Darwin usually celebrated Thanksgiving at the cottage. Carl was invited to attend this year.

"Darwin? His first name is Darwin?" Carl asked.

"It is a bit odd," Joyce agreed. "I'll let him tell you about it."

"Won't it be too cold up north by Thanksgiving?" Carl asked.

"Not in Canada," Joyce replied with a smile. "Our Thanksgiving is much earlier than the American one."

"Do you still eat turkey?" he asked, half picturing a huge fireplace with a whole moose turning on a spit.

"Yes, but we don't go shopping the day after," she said and poked him in the ribs.

Chapter 46

Royal Flush

The best of hands in a game with no wild cards, it is a hand with 10, Jack, Queen, King, and Ace all of which are of the same suit. This is as good as it gets.

Thanksgiving on Lake Simcoe was Carl's first taste of Canadian cottage life. It was not as he had pictured it. He had expected a log cabin, or at least a small rustic house, by the side of a beaver pond with an old dock and a canoe.

Instead, he found that Clive and Ellen had a two-story mansion with three decks extending out over a bay which opened on a lake so large he couldn't see the other side. There was a hot tub on one deck, a lap pool on the lowest deck with a wet bar beside it and a sauna at one end.

The boathouse had slips for two large boats. An 18 foot bow rider was sitting on a sling above one and a 26 foot sailboat with its mast unstepped sat in a custom dry dock at the other side. A guest room, a self-contained apartment above the boathouse, had a spectacular view over the long bay on which the property backed. The boathouse, which was set to one side of the large waterfront lot so as not to block the view from the main cottage, was accessible by a path which led up to the lowest deck.

Joyce informed Carl that they had been given the use of the boathouse apartment to themselves for the weekend so they could have some privacy. Apparently he had met with familial approval.

The property, on the western shore of Lake Couchiching, was near the town of Orillia, which Carl learned had been the town upon which the Canadian humourist, Stephen Leacock, had based a series of stories *Sunshine Sketches of a Little Town.* In the stories Leacock had called the town Mariposa, Carl soon discovered, because he was presented with a copy of the book upon arrival. Apparently this was a traditional welcome to guests practiced by Clive and Ellen.

Since it was a warm day and the water was very calm, Clive lowered the bow rider into the water and took Joyce and Carl for a ride down to "The Narrows" which forms part of the Trent waterway. From here a boat could go north through Lake Couchiching and then descend a series of locks to Georgian Bay or by crossing Lake Simcoe, take another series of locks and lakes to the eastern end of Lake Ontario.

Dinner was turkey, not moose, though the fireplace in front of which they sat after dinner was big enough for a spit to cook a moose.

The chat by fireside was light and relaxed until Darwin posed a few questions about politics. Carl wasn't strongly political, but he had been taught by his mother to respect all points of view. He told Darwin that he felt sad when he saw people who wanted to work but couldn't find work. That was one thing he had thought seemed good in Cuba. If someone was willing to work there was a job for him.

Darwin said "A lot better than breadlines, eh?" Then Darwin became a bit more direct. He said he thought all bankers and lawyers were crooks.

Clive interrupted what seemed to a burgeoning rant from Darwin to explain to Carl that Darwin thought they should have a revolution in Canada and kill all the rich.

Darwin laughed at that and said if that were the case, Clive would be one of the first up against the wall.

Clive admitted that he had done alright for himself, but that he had earned it honestly.

"If you call the stock market honest," Darwin rejoined.

Clive explained, for Carl's benefit, that he was a retired stock broker.

"It's hard to make money in the market, Carl," Clive said. "Unless you're getting paid whether it goes up or down."

Carl asked Darwin about his name. It seemed an unusual first name.

"It certainly is," Darwin agreed. "But my second name is worse. Can you guess what it might be?"

"Well," said Carl "I would guess 'Charles,' but that doesn't seem so bad."

"Nor would it be," Clive chimed in. "Our father had a strange sense of humour. Darwin's second name is 'Beagle,' as in the ship."

"The ship Charles Darwin traveled on to the Galapagos Islands?"

"The same," Darwin said with a wide grin.

"Can you imagine being saddled with 'Beagle' as a name?" Clive asked. "It's worse than Clive."

Carl wanted to tell them about his own birth name, Wolfgang Amadeus, but couldn't. For neither the first, nor the last time, he felt the constraint of secrecy.

A discussion of investments with Clive led Carl to the realization that the same cautious approach and research which Clive advocated for investment should be a part of his planning for the contractual arrangement he undertook for Stan. You might at least want to make sure there are no other gunmen around, he chided himself, remembering the near disaster of Altoona.

Chapter 47

Stud Poker

A game of poker in which you don't get to draw or exchange cards. You play what you are dealt.

Later that night he held Joyce in his arms and said "I like your family."

"They like you too," Joyce responded. "I could tell that."

"Ellen is your aunt by marriage, isn't she?"

"Yes," Joyce told him. "My only relatives on my mother's side are in England. And even they are only cousins and second cousins."

"I'm never sure what the difference is between second cousin and cousin twice removed," said Carl. "In my case it doesn't matter. I have no family at all."

"Does that make you sad?" Joyce asked.

"I'm not sure," Carl replied. "I've never known any different."

They fell asleep in each other's arms.

It was the best Thanksgiving Carl had ever spent.

Chapter 48

Draw Poker

A variation of poker in which you can throw away some cards and have them replaced by the dealer.

Joyce and Carl went to Europe again the summer of 1988. This time they flew into Munich and visited Southern Germany castles, Austrian resorts, including Zell am See, and drove through the Alps to northern Italy where they discovered a wonderful hotel on the shore of Lago de Garda at Torri del Benaco. They were both open to trying all the local food and wine and loved the excitement of searching out new places to see.

They circled back to Munich by way of Switzerland and decided that they would make a special visit to Venice as soon as they could.

By this time they both know they wanted to be together. Neither of them wanted to have children. It was not that they disliked children, they just didn't feel the need.

For Carl it was at least partly that he knew that he might be killed, or worse arrested, sometime and he did not want to have a son or daughter if he wasn't going to be there as a father. This was probably because of his own family experience, Carl thought. Understanding the cause didn't change the feeling, however. He just knew that he would rather not take on the responsibility.

Joyce had made her own decision not to have children for reasons he didn't question. Whatever the explanation, the result was that they were both content to live their lives without raising a family. Some people would say they were selfish, but if you don't care for yourself, who would you care for? Carl asked himself. Wasn't there a book, *The Selfish Gene,* which showed how important it was to take care of yourself?

Some people are selfless. Mother Teresa might be one of these.

Others are self absorbed. This list is endless with persons such as Paris Ritz or Rome Hilton, or whatever that person's name was, Carl could never bother remembering.

Many are self conscious, or self pitying, or self important. It seemed innocent enough to be selfish.

Carl decided to ask Joyce to marry him. With typical attention to detail, he set up an elaborate scenario which would have the ring brought out to her with dessert at a dinner together in September.

The fact that his clever plan came unraveled served as a warning to Carl. It's hard enough to do something yourself; don't rely on another person as part of any complex plan. 'Pass me the gun now, Harry. What do you mean you forgot to load it?'

The fact that Joyce accepted him anyway was a testament to her low expectations more than anything, Carl teased himself.

Chapter 49

Straight Seven

Players are each dealt seven cards. Variations exist. The most common has two cards face down, four cards face up, and a seventh card down.

It's been a long time since we met in Cuba. But who's counting, thought Carl. The next three years were filled with joy of life and adventures together for Joyce and Carl. It was in late September of 1989 that Carl asked Joyce to marry him.

She accepted and they set a date for the following spring.

They would honeymoon in Italy. But maybe not Sicily, thought Carl.

Joyce was getting started in real estate and Carl was well established as a reliable agent for Stan. He was attending Brock part-time and working from home on the computer as a business analyst. He would later call himself a business consultant, but at 25 it was a bit of a sell to make anyone think he had the experience to be a consultant.

In fact, he probably could have helped many people who thought they were in business but were really just running through the net worth of a business they had inherited. Carl was good at recognizing a good investment. The money he earned went into solid investments in Spain, where he had recognized land opportunities, India, where the call centres and programme writing was getting under way, and a new area which was just taking off, high tech and on-line gambling.

A lot of the established crime families had made their fortunes in Vegas. On-line was the new Vegas. Carl made some sizable investments in on-line poker sites and took out most of his money after it had more than doubled in two years.

Even a small investment will grow well with good returns, and Carl was always careful to keep his investments small and spread around.

His intention was to continue to work and to increase the diversity of his investments.

His annual net income from his main job was over $200,000 and he declared only $50,000 of that. By continuing to increase his net worth by approximately $150,000 per year plus interest, Carl could look forward to surpassing $1,000,000 in assets within six years. After that he was set.

It was a simple matter of spending less than you made, and making much more than you needed. Carl was good at handling money and he wasn't greedy. He invested only where it was safest. There was a saying he had heard applied to the stock market: Sometimes the bulls win, sometimes the bears win, but the pigs always lose.

This saying could apply even to bonds. If the rate of return was very high, it usually was because underlying risk was high too. It didn't matter how high the promised interest was if the bond became worthless.

There had been a number of "investment specialists" in the Niagara Region who had promised high returns on investment and turned out to be Ponzi artists who used new investments to pay off older ones until the money ran out.

Chapter 50

Going Head to Head

Term used to describe two players facing off against each other.

As it turned out, Joyce and Carl spent their honeymoon in Spain in 1990. Though neither was especially religious, they visited the cathedrals of Toledo, Seville, and Barcelona. The cathedrals in Toledo and Seville are the third and fourth largest after St Peter's in Rome and St. Paul's in London, the brochures informed them. They were certainly magnificent.

But the cathedral under construction in Barcelona from the designs of Gaudi was the most memorable. It had been under construction for 100 years and would be another 50 before completion, they were told. When the huge cross is mounted on top, the structure will dominate all of Barcelona, Carl imagined.

Joyce and Carl were touched by the special symbol they found in Toledo of the Crescent Moon of the Moors, the Christian cross, and the Star of David entwined in one symbol of faith and tolerance. How ironic that Toledo should come to be the seat of terror during the dark days of the Spanish Inquisition. No one expects the Spanish Inquisition, thought Carl.

They spent six weeks there and traveled through much of the country. The food and wine was less spectacular than France or Italy, but the warmth of the people and the special character of the night life charmed them both.

They stayed in *paradors*, medieval castles restored and turned into state-run hotels. They visited other monuments to Moorish architecture: the Alhambra and Santa Catalina in Granada and Jaen. They drove the winding mountain roads and went up a cable car to a peak in the Sierra Nevada from whence they could see the wine dark Mediterranean Sea.

They attended a summer concert set in the natural caves at Nerja and sipped *vino tinto* of Rioja on the *Balcon de Europa* where it thrust out into the sea.

They stumbled upon a small wine bodega in Malaga, *Taverna de la Guarda*, which was magical. Huge barrels of sweet blended wines of Muscat and Pedro Ximenes grapes from the highlands behind Malaga were served across trellis tables by impish characters out of Dickens with crimson noses, ruddy faces and sparkling eyes. The charges for the wines they ordered and the fresh seafood finger foods were written in chalk upon the tables near them to be erased with a cloth when settled up.

The beaches were alive with people and seaside restaurants which served fresh linguado and deep fried calamari. The mountain towns, where only a few decades ago Franco's forces had battled republicans, preserved their secrets and their charms. One town especially, Camares, with its view of the hills and the sea captivated their spirit.

They vowed to return there together some day.

Chapter 51

Hit Me

In blackjack the term is used to ask for another card.

Obviously it has a second, more sinister, meaning as well.

In early October of 1990, Stan offered Carl a contract on a drug dealer in North Las Vegas. Most tourists who visit the casinos in Las Vegas think it is a safe city. It is safe near the Casino Strip. The people who make their money from the casinos make sure that the areas where the cash cows, the tourists, go are safe. They keep the wolves out of the pasture.

There was a robbery of one of the casinos once. The crime was never solved by the police. Carl was sure the robbers were taken care of privately. Their bodies were never found. Most crooks were smart enough not to mess around near the strip.

North Las Vegas, on the other hand, had more violent crime than almost any other American City. Houston is right up there too when it comes to rough stuff.

In a violent city an outlaw tends to watch out for trouble. So it was with "John" the pusher. "John" was not a nice man. He ran prostitutes who he kept strung out and frightened. He supplied some of the nastier drugs to addicts and occasionally had someone beaten up or killed by his group of thugs.

I should get a medal for taking this one out, thought Carl. I'm probably saving lives by doing so. I'm using a gun as a form of prophylactic.

This would be a difficult and potentially dangerous hit. There was no doubt that "John" would be protected and difficult to get to. He also wore body armor when out and about. This would require something special.

Carl couldn't count on getting close enough to "John" to use a .22 to the head. A head shot might be a good choice, but Carl needed to use something with a little more power in case he had to put a bullet where it might run into a Kevlar vest.

He shot the Colt ACP .45 regularly in IPSC pistol competitions, but he didn't like the way it threw spent brass about. The gun had some good points. The barrel on the semi automatic could be easily changed to deflect laboratory analysis. The gun itself is a beautiful design. In 1911 Colt produced it to submit to the U.S. Army in response to a request for a sidearm with knock down power. The gun Colt produced won the competition. It had been so well designed that, except for a couple safety devices, it has remained unchanged since then.

It is a very safe gun. It can only be fired by holding the grip to depress the safety on the handle and squeezing the trigger. It will not fire if dropped on the ground when loaded because of a fail-safe drop-down safety block for the firing pin. Even if the gun were in a fire, the exploding bullet would only go down the barrel if a round had been jacked into the firing chamber.

That being said, the slug from a .45 will knock someone down and kill very well. When the slug is metal jacketed and Teflon coated, it will penetrate body armor.

The caliber would suit Carl's needs. The gun to shoot it in which best suited his needs was the S&W .45 revolver. Although the revolver held only five rounds, the power it packed was such that that it would do the job if you can hit what you aim at.

Carl went in carrying his .38 snubnose and the .45. He had spent two full weeks scouting "John" carefully while keeping a low profile.

He had decided that the bodyguard would have to go too. No extra charge, Stan.

"John" was in the alley behind one of his crack houses when Carl took him out. These people spend a lot of time in alleys, Carl thought. It must be annoying to the rats and cats that live there.

He had time to aim with the first shot, so he took the bodyguard out with a head shot. He knocked "John" down with a gut shot that may very well have been a killer itself but he made sure with another shot into the back of the head from his .38. It wouldn't hurt to have people discover two different size slugs and think there were two shooters. That might help cloud any follow-up.

It all made a hell of a lot of noise. Carl was into his rental car and out of the alley before anyone came out to investigate. He didn't think anyone would want to hurry out to what had to sound like a serious gun fight, even though his were the only three shots fired. But he didn't hang around to find out.

He drove straight to the car rental lot and left the car parked there. He dropped the keys through a slit in the door. They would charge his, Calvin's, credit card and be happy to find that they could add an extra charge for filling up the tank.

Car rental agencies like to keep their cars on the road. They would clean up the car and have it rented to someone else before the police even found someone who might have seen the car leaving the scene. Not that Carl thought the police would find anyone who could see straight or would tell them anything.

Carl took a cab to the strip and entered his hotel, the Gold Nugget, through the casino. Actually the only way in and out of most Las Vegas hotels was through the casino. He went to his room, turned on the T.V. and took a cold beer from the fridge.

He slept well and had a hearty breakfast. He decided that there was no point looking at the morning newspaper. Reporting murders in town was not in the interests of the hotels or casinos. Local reporters knew that and stuck to less controversial news stories.

Using a throwaway phone, Carl called Joyce and told her that his meetings in New York were almost over and he would be home in a day or so. He drove to Tucson and flew home from there. He liked Tucson. He established a safety deposit box there for his tools because he might visit again.

Carl imagined that North Las Vegas had a replacement for "John" on the street before his flight out of Tucson touched down in Buffalo. If the police hadn't closed the case they were probably not sitting up at night worrying about who had taken "John" out.

He'd kept in contact with Joyce while away and was very happy to get back home. She asked him how his work in New

York had gone and he said all was fine. He thought from now on his work with that investment firm could be done online.

He actually had an investment broker he dealt with in New York who was a good name to drop whenever anyone asked anything about his business there. Carl found that most people's eyes tend to glaze over fairly quickly if you talk in depth about municipal bond offerings and the importance of convertible bonds versus strip bonds and debentures. Carl could probably lecture about investment ladders and balancing portfolios of derivative-based investments. A recording of such a lecture could serve as an aid to insomnia.

It was his personal opinion that no one really understood derivatives and he seldom invested his own money in anything more risky than government bonds from a variety of federal, provincial, and municipal sources from a number of fairly solvent countries.

No investment is totally safe, he thought. He didn't even trust paper money, but it was hard to get gold coins in banks these days or to use them to buy things. One of these days, he thought the computers will all crash and the finances of the world will go into chaos with them. Hope it's not too soon.

Meanwhile he would try to diversify his investments and build up some reserves in various banks and countries.

Chapter 52

Dealer's Call

In some games, various types of poker may be played in accordance with the choice of the person dealing that hand.

Carl had been shaken by seeing Ronnie. He didn't think Ronnie had seen him, or at least not recognized him. It was a long time.

Yeah, it was a long time since he had seen Ronnie too, but he'd known it was him in a second. He still had the same weasel-like expression. His narrow pointed nose separated the same shifty eyes. Yes, it was a cliché, but it was one Ronnie lived down to. Ronnie had never been trusted, by anyone, and with good reason. He couldn't even be trusted to do what was often in his own best interest. He was always looking for an edge, a way to take a short cut or to short change or over charge someone.

How had he come to be working for Mr. Rizzo in Lewiston? And what did that say about Mr. Rizzo who had employed such a slime ball?

Carl thought of Stan. Stan would probably know something about Mr. Rizzo, especially if he was actively involved in the kinds of things that the people Stan knew were actively involved in. Carl wanted to talk to Stan anyway about retiring. He'd see what Stan could tell him about Mr. Rizzo and Ronnie.

It was Friday. Joyce was at work and he felt like a drive to clear his head.

The ice-cream store in Niagara-on-the-Lake was open. Friday evenings he and Joyce usually took the evening off for some quality bonding. Maybe a movie and some ice cream would go well. Carl stopped in and ordered a hand-packed tub of spumoni ice cream.

No use letting the spumoni melt while waiting to get through to Stan and let him get to a safe phone. He paid for it and asked them to keep it in the freezer for him while he ran an errand.

He went across to use a public phone near the old courthouse theatre. It took a few minutes to get Stan on a safe line. When he did, Stan was eager to offer him a hit in the Finger Lakes.

At any other time Carl would have been pleased to consider it. Now all he could think of was disengaging.

Stan started out with a pitch for Carl taking on the hit in New York State. Stan even started going on about how good the wines of the Finger Lake region were becoming and recommended a restaurant. It sounded as if he were doing some tourism promo work on the side.

Stan was beginning to wax almost poetic in his description of what a simple hit it would be to take out the punk who had set up a small time drug and credit card operation in the bucolic suburbs of the charming little town, Penn Yan.

Carl tried to think of ways to gently turn the conversation to Ronnie.

Or, I could just cut to the chase, he thought.

"I'm sorry Stan. I'd like to help you out, but I've got a bit of a concern about a mutual acquaintance from years ago," he told Stan.

"Who is that?" Stan asked, suddenly all business.

"Do you remember a guy called Ronnie? I think his last name was Mac-something."

"Ronnie Mackenzie!" Stan responded after a second. "Yeah, I remember him. You couldn't trust him to go across the street for a paper. What about him?"

"Well, I think I may have seen him driving a limo." He paused not wanting to tie himself into where he actually lived. "It was at the Buffalo airport," Carl added. "I was catching a connecting flight." Carl forced himself to stop elaborating before the whole story took on a storybook quality.

"I wouldn't be surprised," Stan said with a laugh. "He was useless as a crook. He probably took a job as a cabby."

"No, it wasn't a livery service. It looked like a private limo. He was dressed up like a chauffeur and there was some nattily attired Italianate gentleman getting out of it."

"Nattily, Italianate," Stan echoed. "Are you turning into one of those 'effete intellectuals' Spiro Agnew was always on about?"

"Sorry," Carl said with a laugh. "Should I have said a spiffy spic or a well-dressed WOP?"

"Nah, I understood. I'll look into it if you like. Is he a problem for you?"

"Not yet," Carl said and left it at that. "Can I call you back on this?"

"Sure give me a call on 3 at 5:00 my time. Are you near the New York time zone?"

"Near enough that it's no problem," Carl told him. Carl was always careful about giving away his location, even with Stan. He hung up and thought about why he hadn't mentioned retiring. Let's take this one step at a time. I may need to keep my connections intact for a little longer. Carl remembered what a friend from his university days used to say: "We'll burn that bridge when we get to it."

He hadn't seen the Flop yet and he would like to consider his hole cards before committing himself to much. Ronnie may not have even noticed him.

He picked out a movie for tonight from the video store. They'd both seen The Illusionist when it first came out, but Joyce had mentioned seeing it again and he was up for that. They had both found it a spiritually uplifting movie. With the exception of the pretender to the throne, the characters were warm and caring. He could do with a little uplifting of his spirits right now.

He drove home and prepared a casserole for their supper. He put it in the oven and set the timer to start at 4:00. The one dish meal would be ready when Joyce got home at 5:30. Friday's they had a quick end-of-week meeting at the office.

At 4:40 he checked on the oven and headed out to the nearest public phone which was in Queenston. With everyone carrying mobiles it was getting harder to find a public phone.

Stan answered on the first ring. "Yeah?"

"It is el lobo," Carl responded. He still identified himself as Wolf with Stan. It was how Stan knew him; it worked for them.

"I checked on our friend," Stan began without preamble. "He's got a regular job driving for a Mr. Rizzo in Lewiston. He must have been taking him to the airport when you saw Ronnie."

"Rizzo's not a player?" Carl asked.

"Not as such," Stan responded. "He has some familial connections, but he's got a large construction company that actually does business."

"Okay, that's fine. I just wondered," Carl said. "I'm planning to make a life change and I don't want any loose ends."

"Life change? Like getting married?" Stan asked.

Living as Carl did was difficult. Maybe that was one reason he felt it was time to kill the killer in him. He needed to become a single individual. Stan didn't know that Carl was already married. Carl had had to keep that detail private too.

More than once he had wanted to share that wonderful part of his life with the one person who knew what he did to earn money. Stan was aware of that side of Carl, but Carl could not take the risk of letting him see the rest of him.

Instead he maintained the distance. "Maybe even that. Mainly I've decided to retire."

There was a short silence. Then Stan surprised Carl by saying "Good for you!"

"You're not going to try to talk me out of it?"

"Hell, no," Stan said with a laugh. "I'm happy for you. You're getting out while you're on top. I may retire some day myself."

Carl paused. Then he said, "Thank you. That means a lot to me."

"Take care, my friend," Stan said and they hung up.

As Carl walked back to his car he felt as if he was walking into a bright, new world.

Chapter 53

A Break in the Action

In a tournament it is common to have scheduled breaks to allow players to unwind, at least temporarily.

Joyce was delighted by the choice of movie. Carl was dying to tell her of his decision to stop killing for a living, though he could not say exactly that. Carl was excited by the prospect of a future unsullied by having to keep secrets from her.

The casserole was simple, the bottle of Chardonnay was simple, the evening they had planned was simple, but Carl felt as if life was wonderful.

He wanted to share his feelings with Joyce.

Over supper he said, "I've been going over our financial position."

"And?"

"We have enough money," he said simply.

"Enough for what?"

"Enough to do whatever we want to do without working, within reason," he told her with a smile.

Joyce just looked at him for a moment. Then she said, "I want to live in a castle in Spain."

"As long as it's a small castle, we can do that."

"Can we have a drawbridge?"

"Yes, and a moat," Carl told her. "Is that really what you want?"

"Well, after last winter I've been thinking that it would be nice to be somewhere warm during the winter months. Snow is pretty, but I'm getting tired of driving through it."

"What about your work?" Carl asked. He had wondered how she would react to the idea of change. A lot of people see themselves as their work. He didn't, he thought Joyce didn't either, but he hadn't been sure.

"I enjoy my work, but I could just as easily do something else. I assume that running a castle, even a small one, would take some time," she said with a laugh.

"Well, I'm serious. If you are open to the idea, I would like to consider looking for something in Andalusia. We could easily afford something there and the weather is good."

Joyce stood up and came around the table. She put her hands on his shoulders and kissed him on the neck. "Let's do it. Let's start looking. As long as we can afford to pay the bills, I'll be happy with a very small castle."

They moved into the living room with a glass of wine and spent an hour talking about what they would like in a location and in a structure. It felt like planning to play house.

Both wanted to be near or at least have a view of water. They wanted to be on a hill with a view, especially of sunset. Joyce wanted a bit of land where they could have a small garden. Carl wanted a small shed where he could have a workshop. They decided that being on the edge of a small village would be best so that they could walk to a store if they wanted to.

"Do you remember that hill town near Malaga where we stayed on our honeymoon?" Carl asked.

"The one with the hotel run by a gay couple?"

"That's it. Remember the views from there?"

"I remember a lot of wonderful things about that town," Joyce replied with a twinkle in her eye.

They talked on and on making plans and remembering. The movie went unwatched. The ice cream went uneaten. They went to bed early and began life anew in each other's arms.

Chapter 54

Putting the Stacks in Order

Players are required to arrange their stack of chips such that their opponents can see how much they have.

Saturday, Joyce had an open house to supervise. She left early to pick up some signs from the office and some doughnuts to greet the potential buyers who would wander through.

Carl spent an hour looking over websites of property for sale in Spain. He intended to also prepare a spreadsheet to show Joyce the extent of their investments and a budget which would provide financial security without either of them working.

He would convert some of his investments into an annuity and with the care he had always taken, spread risk to ensure that Joyce would be secure even if he died.

At least the chance of me being shot will diminish, he thought.

He and Joyce had decided to plan an extended stay in Spain for the upcoming winter. They'd take their time looking at properties available while visiting likely regions of Andalusia. Joyce would talk to her fellow workers at the office and arrange to turn over her contacts to other agents at the firm. She would complete her present commitments but then would resign.

He had the Michelin route finder website open and was checking distances between towns in the south of Spain when the phone rang.

He picked it up casually and said, "Hello."

The response almost stopped his heart.

"Hello, Wolf."

Chapter 55

Raising the Stakes

The level of the Blinds goes up during the tournament according to a schedule. This forces the game to an end with one winner.

Carl knew who it was. It was Ronnie.

As had been said many times, The jig was up.

Knowing it was useless, Carl said, "I'm afraid you have the wrong number."

"That won't work, Wolf," Ronnie said in the same annoying voice which Carl remembered from days in the 'hood. "I know your new name; I know where you live; and I know that you've been shooting people for Stan. It's just like the old days."

Carl sat back in his chair and looked at the picture of Spain on his computer screen.

"Well, nice of you to call, Ronnie. I see you've got a real job too."

"Cut the crap, Wolf. You know why I'm calling," Ronnie snarled.

"Not just to say hi?" Carl asked, keeping his voice controlled while his mind raced.

"I know that you don't want your wife and the police to find out who you really are," Ronnie continued. "I can keep my mouth shut."

"Then we don't have a problem," Carl told him.

"That's right, except you've got money and I want some to keep quiet."

"Why wouldn't I just kill you?" Carl asked. He knew that even Ronnie would have known that was an option. He wanted to 'cut the crap' too.

There was a pause while Ronnie absorbed the direct statement. He must have known it was a possibility. Carl fully expected what he heard next.

"Don't even think about that shit. I've left instructions for what I know to be made public if something happens to me," Ronnie said, his voice tight with tension.

Carl didn't believe him. Ronnie was bluffing. But the risk in calling the bluff directly was too high so he would have to approach this another way.

"What do you want from me?" he asked.

"$50,000," Ronnie said. "For fifty grand, I'll keep my mouth shut."

Carl knew that if he paid Ronnie $50,000, it would just lead to more demands later. The trick was to keep Ronnie from realizing that Carl knew. He had to delay things until he could work out a permanent solution.

"I don't have $50,000," Carl responded. He knew that Ronnie would expect him to say that. He wanted to seem predictable.

"You can raise it. You can borrow it; you can mortgage your house. Just do it!" Ronnie demanded.

"That will take time."

"I'll give you a week." Even Ronnie must realize that he was being unreasonable, Carl thought.

"I can't do anything today. I'll talk to my bank on Monday, but it might take some time to raise that kind of money."

"I'll call back on Monday. You'd better do it," Ronnie told him.

Carl was almost amused by how bad Ronnie was at this.

"Monday's too soon for me to have an answer from the bank. Call me Tuesday afternoon at 4:00," he told Ronnie in a tone that he hoped sounded convincing. "But don't call me on this line. I'll give you my mobile number."

Ronnie agreed to call Tuesday and Carl gave him the number of one of the throw-away mobiles which he used.

As he hung up the phone, he reflected on how easily things turn to rat shit.

Chapter 56

Fish or Cut Bait

Although equally applicable to life as poker, there comes a time when you have to commit or back off.

All Saturday evening while he and Joyce had a quiet meal and watched the movie, Carl's mind had been racing. He felt as if he were outside his body directing it to be normal and natural while he turned one fantastical plan after another over in his mind.

Ironically, the solution came to him while they were watching The Illusionist. He had to disappear.

We all have the same goals in life, he thought. We want to be safe and happy.

The main characters in the movie could not hope to just run away because they would be pursued as long as people knew they were alive. His problem was somewhat the same. He needed a way to drop out of sight and have Joyce join him. But he also needed a way to prevent Ronnie revealing all.

If he didn't exist, Ronnie would have nothing to blackmail Joyce with. If Ronnie didn't exist, there would be no one to threaten. How could that be arranged?

Could he adapt the solution in the movie to fit his situation? He thought he could.

Chapter 57

Call, Raise, or All-in

Once you decide to commit to a pot you can make a Call to close off the size of the bet; you can Raise to either get more or drive the other player(s) out; or you can make a total commitment and go All-in.

By Sunday morning Carl knew what he must do. He was not going to let Ronnie control him. He would put everything he had on the line, win or lose.

He told Joyce that he needed to visit their boat *Reflections* to prepare her for the winter. There might be time for one more cruise on the river, but most of the winter preparation should be done now before there was the risk of freezing.

Joyce offered to come with him. He was happy to have the company.

They drove up to the marina through a crisp, sunny day. Winter was in the air. Football season was upon them. Carl planned to watch Buffalo at New England this afternoon. Some of the poker group were planning to go to the Buffalo home game next Sunday against New York. He'd probably miss that.

It didn't take long to do what needed to be done with the boat. He had already had the holding tank pumped out and now he reduced the water in the potable water tank and added a bit of biodegradable antifreeze.

Joyce and he removed some things which might suffer damage from freezing temperatures and stored everything else away so that the boat could be lifted out and shrink wrapped for storage.

Carl wanted to make an adjustment to the anchor rode shackle, so he removed that and took it home to his workshop. *Reflections* was a good boat. He would miss her.

Chapter 58

Over Call

When someone else has demonstrated a willingness to bet on a hand by Calling, it is sometimes useful to make a larger bet, an Over Call, in an attempt to force the opposition out of the hand.

Tuesday dawned clear and sunny. What a beautiful day for late September.

Joyce was off early to show a house to a prospect from Toronto. Carl made sure that he had everything he needed for his errands across the river. He drove slowly toward the border crossing. There was no hurry.

As was his habit, Carl glanced up and down the river as he crossed the Queenston/Lewiston Bridge into the U.S. The view was spectacular.

Up river from the bridge the water swirled with undercurrents from the discharge from the giant turbines of the Hydro Electric generators. Down river the waters regrouped and flowed on slowly. Here I am, suspended between past and future, Carl thought. Will things smooth out for me? Yes, one way or another, he concluded.

A quotation from one of his courses came back to him. It was attributed to the ancient philosopher Thales: "No man steps in the same river twice." Things change and the swirl and eddies of life carry some of us swiftly down stream while others drift to the shore.

Or float belly up into the turbine intakes, he thought grimly.

The air was clear and tranquil, a trace of summer's warmth lingered, but a few leaves had turned and the threat of what was to come brooded.

It is time to put things in order for the uncertainty to come, Carl thought.

He had a few things to do to get ready for tonight. He would pick up some cheese at Premier, maybe some pate as well. He wanted to make another quick call to Stan. There were the guns he had stored in a safety deposit box to pick up. He would be near Lewiston when Ronnie called. He wanted to get to the meeting point before Ronnie.

He had prepared a package for Ronnie which he would either give to him in person or leave with someone for him to pick up.

After he finished with Ronnie he would drive up the American side on the river road. There was a lookout over the power plant which was perfect for dropping something heavy into depths of turbulent water. No recreational scuba diver would come across anything lying on the bottom there.

Then he would cross the Rainbow Bridge into Niagara Falls, Canada and visit *Reflections*. He wanted to ensure that the battery was fully charged and she was ready to do what he needed of her.

Carl drove into Buffalo and picked up the cheese and pate for the poker game. It was at Tom's tonight and he had promised to bring some good European cheeses.

On an impulse he also bought a jar of Cumberland sauce. It would go well with both the cheese and pate. Live it up, he thought. What was it Bugs Bunny used to say? "Hare today, goon tomorrow." Life is too short to drink bad wine or eat inferior food if you have a choice, he had decided long ago.

No need to take unnecessary risks though, he added. He put the cheese and pate into a thermal cooler with the frozen ice pack he had brought with him. Carl was always careful. Dying tonight of food poisoning would be just too ironic.

After he picked up the guns he drove slowly back toward Lewiston. He stopped at a gas station on the way and used their public phone to call Stan. He had to wait again for Stan to go to one of his safe phones, so he had a BLT and a cherry coke at the snack bar.

When he connected with Stan he filled him in on the situation with Ronnie and asked a favour. He wanted to be sure that no matter what happened tonight there would be no lingering problem for Joyce.

Stan expressed his opinion of Ronnie again. He agreed with Carl that Ronnie could not be trusted and promised to do what was needed to make sure he caused no future problems.

Chapter 59

Big Slick

Holding the hole-cards, Ace and King, is referred to as Big Slick. If the two cards are of the same suit, 'suited,' it is considered by many as more powerful than a pair of aces because of its potential for improvement.

Carl had given Ronnie the number of a throw away mobile he had bought at a K-Mart. Ronnie was the only person who had this number and was the only person Carl would ever speak to on it. That phone rang at one minute after four.

He's eager, Carl reminded himself. Don't over play your hand. Let him think you are desperate but wanting to do business.

"I'm here," he said.

"Do you have the money?"

"We need to talk about that," Carl replied.

"There's nothing to talk about. Pay me $50,000 or I expose you. How would your wife react to that? What about the police? I'll bet there are even some people you've hit who have friends who might like to look you up," Ronnie's voice was tense. He's worried. Don't push too hard. Just make it seem as normal as such a situation can be.

"Listen. I just want to settle this. I can't get $50,000 in cash right away. I assume you don't want a cheque?" he said as sincerely as he could make it sound.

"Damn right I don't want a cheque. How much can you get right away?"

"I've got $10,000 in U.S. currency. I'll give that to you now and I can get the rest in one or two months. But I want it clear that after the $50,000 you never contact me again," Carl told him.

Carl knew that whatever Ronnie promised wouldn't be worth a tinker's damn. He'd always wondered about the origin of that saying, but perhaps right now he should stay focused, he reminded himself.

"How will I get the money?" Ronnie replied.

I probably could have got him to agree to less, Carl thought. But since Ronnie would never see a second payment it didn't matter much.

"I've got it with me," Carl said. "I can bring it to you. I'm in Buffalo," he told Ronnie.

"We don't need to meet," Ronnie responded.

"Well, what do you want me to do, leave it on a park bench?"

Ronnie didn't answer for a few seconds. What a moron, Carl thought. He hasn't reasoned this out at all.

Finally Ronnie said, "Okay, meet me at the Brickyard in Lewiston. It's a bar on the main street. But don't try anything. I've got friends there who will be watching."

As if, Carl amused himself by thinking. I could probably shoot him standing at the bar and someone would shake my hand and offer to buy me a drink.

It was not part of his plan to let Ronnie think that he had any doubt about what Ronnie told him. So he contented himself by saying "I can be there in 30 minutes."

"Okay. I'll be sitting in a booth at the back. Come alone and don't bring a gun," Ronnie told him.

"Yes. Alright. No problem," Carl reassured him.

This would be so simple if I didn't have to worry about Joyce, he thought. But without Joyce, I don't know what else would seem worthwhile.

Another poem from Edna St. Vincent Milay came back to him. "Love is not all . . ." she starts out, but she goes on to show that it is all that really matters.

Carl had decided that he was willing to risk everything else to have Joyce love him. He had decided that he would have to tell her everything and hope that she would still love him.

Chapter 60

Cowboys

A pair of kings are the second highest pair. As such they are valued. Obviously the appearance of an ace can be disturbing.

In fact, Carl was much closer than 30 minutes away.

Carl drove down to The Brickyard and parked his car half a block away on a side street. Ronnie had seen the Mercedes once and might recognize it.

He walked onto Center St. and into a shop with a clear view of the bar.

Ten minutes after he'd hung up from talking with Ronnie, he was in a gift shop across the street from The Brickyard. Gift shops were perfect for loitering while pretending to be looking for a present for someone. Well, Carl did have a little present for Ronnie. Perhaps he would add a little something to it.

From here he could watch the front and side entrance to The Brickyard and had a view of the entrance to the bar's parking lot which was off the street running behind the bar itself. He wanted to see if Ronnie arrived alone. Unless Ronnie had changed a lot since Carl had known him before, he would be unlikely to have a lot of close friends.

As Carl had expected, Ronnie showed up about ten minutes later. He was driving a grey Mercedes which he parked in the lot. Ronnie was by himself and looking around as he entered the bar by the side door. So much for Ronnie's boast about having back up. Carl could blow him away and probably get away with it. Probably, but Carl wanted to be sure that this play was the last one he had to take a chance on.

If what he had planned worked, he would never have to look over his shoulder again.

Carl waited a good ten minutes more, bought a package of *pot pourri*, and walked across the street to the bar. He wondered if Ronnie would expect what he was going to get.

Carl reminded himself to take it very slowly. Ronnie was probably wound up and could easily panic. It was important that Ronnie feel comfortable and relaxed. Ronnie must believe that Carl was planning to pay him some now and more later.

The fact that Ronnie was planning to ask for even more after that didn't matter.

Get in; get out; drive away, Carl told himself.

Chapter 61

Royal Couple

This slightly romantic name is given to the hole cards, king and queen, when they are of the same suit.

The Brickyard is in an old frame building with some brick veneer facing. It is deeper than it is wide by far and has a long bar along the right side as you walk in. There are booths at the back and one of those machines with small basketballs you can shoot at a hoop to see how many you can score in 60 seconds. Carl walked in by the front door, saw Ronnie sitting at the back watching the door, and walked slowly back to his booth.

In his right hand Carl was carrying a bag from the gift shop with the package he had prepared for Ronnie in it along with the *pot pourri*. He tried to present a non-threatening image.

He slid onto the bench seat across from Ronnie and took control of the conversation. He really disliked Ronnie, he always had; he wanted to keep this as short as possible.

"The money is in a package in this bag. There's no need to open it here. I wouldn't be here if I wasn't prepared to pay you," he told Ronnie. "I'll have the rest of the money in eight weeks."

"Make it six," Ronnie said.

What a fool, Carl thought. As if eight weeks or six made a difference. Never mind, let him think that he's in control.

"I'll try," he said. "Don't call me at home though. Use the same number as today."

"Try hard," Ronnie insisted, "I'll phone you at 4:00 six weeks from today."

You are so close to death as you sit there, Carl mused silently. How I wish I could just point a gun at you right now to teach you a lesson.

"Okay, call then. I'll do what I can," he said.

"We don't need to meet next time," Ronnie told him. "I'll set up a place where you can drop the money."

"That's fine," Carl answered. "I'll get the money for you and then we can both move on."

"Yeah, whatever," Ronnie responded.

Carl got up out of the booth and walked away without looking back. I'll never have to look at him again, he thought.

Chapter 62

Kojak

Holding King and Jack (K, J) occasions a long-in-the-tooth reference to the American television series starring Telly Savalas.

A few minutes later, Carl stood on the lookout over the river. He made sure no one was watching and dropped the guns into the waters below.

He hated to give up these particular revolvers. He had others stashed around the U.S. but this seven-shot S&W .22 was the first of that model that he had owned. It was stainless steel and the years of polishing and cleaning had softened the burnished finish into a warm patina. The other was a snub-nosed, hammerless .38. He didn't think he would ever need either again.

These two were legally registered to him and he could have left them at the club, but he didn't want some bright-eyed, bushy-tailed lab technician doing a random check on them and connecting them with one of many contract hits over the past two decades. Those guns had a bit of history to them.

After a few years in the river they wouldn't be giving out any incriminating ballistics information even if they were somehow found.

Carl didn't like surprises. He wondered if Ronnie did.

Ronnie would probably be surprised when he opened the package Carl had left for him.

Not only would there be a charming little package of *pot pourri*, the currency in the package was nice, old, and untraceable. Ronnie should be more than happy.

The $10,000 was from a stash Carl kept for his personal use when traveling on business and paying cash for everything. Carl had about $7,000 more that he'd taken out of the deposit box. It was in the car with him. He'd put that in his desk at home.

It could be a surprise for Joyce.

Ronnie would not be a problem for a while at least.

Carl now had to make sure there was no threat to Joyce, no matter how everything else he had planned worked out.

Chapter 63

Hooks

In reference to their fishhook shape, used for two or more Jacks.

Carl had time to check out the river from the American side. He drove into and around the little park on Goat Island. At this time of year, he was the only visitor even on so nice a day. Carl was pleased to find it so deserted and tranquil.

Before driving back out of the park and to the bridge, Carl parked near the water and looked at the river near the brink. Not for the first time he looked with wonder at the glass-like smoothness of the water as it curled over the edge and tumbled down into the gorge.

It was hypnotic and compelling. More than one person had plunged to their death over this waterfall which separated the two countries. On the other hand, a few times over the centuries the water had frozen sold to form an ice bridge which people had walked across.

Carl drove back to Canada and south along the parkway road beside the Falls and then up to the marina.

He checked the electrical cable to *Reflections* and examined her bow and stern lines. Everything was fine. He intended to go out once more before having her lifted out of the water for the winter. If she was to be moved to Niagara-on-the-Lake next year it would be done in the spring. There was no need to arrange that now.

As he drove home to change for poker, Carl realized that he had left the companionway door unlatched. Joyce and he had some electronics equipment on board which they usually took home for the winter. He had intended to take it home now.

Well, it didn't matter. They had good insurance which would replace anything on board. Still, he had meant to take it home now, and he didn't like forgetting even small details.

Don't start getting sloppy now, he thought.

Chapter 64

The Blinds

Mandatory bets are required by the two players to the left of the dealer. These bets are referred to as 'Blinds" because they are made without the players seeing their down cards first. The big Blind is twice as large as the small Blind.

Carl was the Big Blind for the first hand of the night. As he put in his bet he reflected on the similarity to doing this to some actions in life. Sometimes you have to commit to something without knowing what will happen.

His marriage had been that. He had been in love with Joyce and was willing to make the commitment, but he had no certain knowledge how it would work out.

He had no regrets on that account, he thought. Marrying Joyce was the best thing he had ever done. Whatever it cost he would do his best to protect her and their relationship. He knew now that he would have to tell Joyce about his work as a hit man and let her decide if she wanted to continue to live with him or not.

Ronnie's threat had made this clear to him; but the truth of it had been there waiting for him to recognize it,

There was a saying that if you love something and let it go, it will come back to you if it loves you. If it doesn't return you must live with that. Well, that wasn't exactly the saying, but it was close enough.

His first hand was a small pair. Uncharacteristically, Carl made a large bet. Everyone else folded and Carl won a small pot. He had decided to change his style tonight. It was never good to become predictable.

The style he was trying on was very aggressive. He bet freely and raised often. It was an approach which could build a large stack quickly, or take him out.

He was building up his stack and was clear chip leader when he came up against Russell.

Carl had a pair of Jacks down. The flop was a two of clubs, a seven of spades, and an ace of diamonds. A flush was unlikely as was a straight, but the ace was potentially dangerous.

Normally Carl would have checked and folded against a large bet. Tonight he raised and then called Russell's all-in.

Russell turned up his hole cards which were an ace and a two.

The turn was a four of hearts which did not help Carl.

The river card was a Queen of spades.

Russell won and became chip leader.

Carl now was small stack. Two hands later he took a plunge on a pair of tens. Before the flop he went all-in. Two players stayed with him: Russell and Tom.

The flop was a three of spades, a seven of spades, and a Jack of clubs.

The two players with money checked.

The turn card was an ace of diamonds.

Both other players checked.

The river card was a four of diamonds.

Both other players checked again.

Tom showed a Jack and five. Russell had two sevens down.

Tom won; Carl was busted out.

As a non-player, he took over as dealer for the table for a while.

Then when Tom was also knocked out, Carl excused himself by saying he needed to run up to his boat because he had left her unlocked. He said he would probably come back to join them before the end.

Tom said he was going to set out the cheese Carl had brought so they could enjoy it as soon as Carl got back.

"I might be about an hour," Carl told him. "I need to run the motor out as well."

Carl went out to his car and drove up toward the marina. It was a clear night. It would be nice out on the river tonight.

Chapter 65

The Flop

After all players have made their initial bets, three cards are placed face up in the middle of the table by the dealer. These cards, called the Flop, are used in common by all the players.

He carefully went through his checklist and prepared the boat. He had learned the importance of a written checklist years ago from Susan's husband, Garth. The flight instructor had many stories of accidents which resulted from failing to properly follow a preflight checklist.

Being careful was equally important in safe boating. It wouldn't do to have the motor fail while he was maneuvering in the current close to the Falls.

Carl checked the motor compartment visually as he always did to ensure that the engine was tilted appropriately. He turned on the electrics, engaged an electric motor, and checked that the I/O drive would raise and lower on command. Then he made sure that it was lowered completely with the transfer gears fully engaged. Before starting the engine he turned the blower on and let it clear the enclosed engine compartment for a full five minutes before starting the engine.

Wouldn't that be ironic, he thought, after all his careful preparations, to have the boat blow up while he was starting the motor. That would be too funny; and he would be the butt of the joke. Carl was not afraid to die, but he had always tried to avoid blowing himself up.

What a stereotypical end for someone who, even he admitted, many would describe as a gangster. "Sure my clients are criminals. I'm a criminal lawyer," one of his lawyer acquaintances had once exclaimed in frustration.

The river was relatively calm and the night, though cool, was clear. The moon was almost full. Visibility on the water would be good and there would be little marine traffic.

The motor started easily and he ran it up a couple times before pulling the throttle back to idle. He turned on his running light and the VHF radio.

Watching his step among the lines he stepped onto the wooden walkway and made his way forward. With practiced familiarity he released the bow line and attached it carefully to the rail with a couple single hitches. He held *Reflections* against the pier as he made his way sternward. He released the stern line and stepped aboard.

There was no wind and the boat floated almost motionless in her mooring. He made a final visual check, engaged the drive in reverse and backed out into the channel.

Carl always enjoyed the passage out through the quiet waters of the channel. A Freudian might suggest a comparison to leaving the birth canal, pun intended, for the dangerous waterways of life. But most Freudians were seriously unbalanced.

As he entered the river proper, he turned up against the current and allowed the boat to angle over toward the American side. As he had expected, he had this section of the river to himself. He wanted to approach the Falls at a point between Goat Island and the Canadian side. If possible he wanted to pass very close to Goat Island where there was a much smaller body of rocks in the river just before the edge.

When he judged that he had maneuvered far enough out into the main current of the river, he allowed the bow to fall off to port and steered straight down the river.

Chapter 66

No Help There

When a card which clearly can have little benefit turns up, the dealer may describe its appearance as "No help there."

OPP Officer L. J. "Snowy" Snow was seated in his cruiser in the parking area near the water intake weirs on the Canadian side. He was taking a well earned break from keeping the highways safe for motorists and finishing off a chocolate walnut crunch doughnut and a double double Tim Horton's coffee.

As he gazed out over the moonlit river he saw a mid-sized cabin cruiser heading down river. "What's that fool doing this close to the rapids," he wondered aloud. One of the few benefits of working alone in a patrol cruiser was the luxury of talking to oneself.

As he watched, the sailor climbed out on the bow deck and appeared to lower the anchor.

Sure enough, he thought, as the craft swung sideways and started to point up river. He must be having engine trouble and be dropping his anchor to hold the boat there. He'll be safe enough if the anchor holds, but we'll have to get help to him. A

Coast Guard inflatable could get to him there with a tow line. I'd better call this in.

He reached toward his radio to call dispatch.

Then the bow jerked up abruptly and the anchor line went slack. He's lost his anchor, "Snowy" thought. This could be serious.

He flashed his lights and opened the door. He half stood and honked his horn. The male figure on the boat heard the horn and waved his hands frantically in the air.

As the boat started to drift downriver again, "Snowy" reached for his microphone.

He called in the report and hoped that dispatch could raise some response. It was nearing 21:00 hrs and it would be difficult to get a lifeline or something across that patch of water near Goat Island. The boat was already far enough into the rapids that a marine rescue would be next to impossible.

Chapter 67

At the Turn

After the Flop another round of betting occurs. When these bets are concluded a fourth card is laid beside the three cards of the Flop. This is called the Turn.

When he was far down river, and directly above the passage of rapids which runs between the two countries, Carl took the next step. He was still quite a ways back from the final, no turning back, point. Here he launched his anchor and felt a certain amount of pride in his preparations as he felt the cable break free releasing the craft to the furious drag of the current.

He heard the blare of a car horn from the Canadian side and saw someone standing by the open door of a car. Carl waved both his arms in the air and tried to look as frantic as possible.

That was a stroke of luck, Carl thought. Whoever that was honking had seen him. There would be a witness that someone had been on the boat.

He had prepared his anchoring system to be faulty. Using a come-along and two trees as end points he had applied stress to the turnbuckle which connected the anchor to the rode until it had snapped. He then reassembled the anchor and rode with the broken turnbuckle and attached it as usual to the Sampson post.

Experts might wonder why the turnbuckle had failed, but it would be clear that it had failed. He had prepared an easy answer for any forensic examiner. That particular turnbuckle, though looking like any other, was a cheap Chinese knock off which could be blamed for the failure. Sorry, comrades, I have to let the chauvinistic capitalist pigs blame you for this one.

He had to be careful navigating here. There were strong currents which could thrust the hull against rock outcroppings in shallows sections. He didn't want to be holed this far up river or to break his prop while he still needed it. He would leave the drive engaged in forward and hope that it would break in a shallow section nearer the edge.

To preserve his drive unit he aimed as best he could for smoother sections of the waterway while trying to stay close to the southern bank. Still waters run deep everyone says; hope that holds true this time, he thought.

A barge had lodged on a shoal very near the Canadian side of the horseshoe section of the Falls. It was surprising that it had never been lifted clear and dragged over the edge. There it remained as a grim reminder of the danger to craft in this section so near the edge.

Carl did not want to have *Reflections* ground herself. If she did, people might think that he had gone overboard in a vain attempt to reach the shore. However, and Carl didn't want this to happen, they might suspect that he hadn't been on board as she drifted toward the edge. If that happened and his body wasn't found, there might be some doubt about whether he had perished or not.

Perish that thought, he amused himself by thinking. He wouldn't want Joyce's inheritance held up by doubts of that sort. It had to be very clear to people that he had plunged over the brink.

To ensure that he was trying to save himself, without actually being rescued, would require precision timing. He would place an emergency call on the VHF radio, and activate the position transmitter which was slaved to his GPS in time for the authorities to confirm that he was on the river and floating toward the edge, but too late for them to reach him.

He had an ace in the hole, so to speak. Whereas he would tell them that he had lost power, he would in fact be propelling the boat toward the drop off point. That way they would have even less time to get to him than they might think.

That was one reason he had to avoid contact with any rocks which could shear off his outboard unit. It would be ridiculous to be spotted pushing off from a grounded position and polling his way toward the edge by some hypothetical observer from the bank.

He adjusted the hydraulic tilt to bring the prop as shallow in the water as possible. Normally the motor tilt was used to trim the boat when cruising, but at slow speed it would keep the prop a little closer to the surface. When he reached the right point on the river he would lower it again.

It was unlikely that on such a cool evening that anyone, no matter how romantically infatuated, would be wandering about on Goat Island. He certainly hoped no one would be in sight of that stretch of water. It was no part of his plan to be rescued or to be believed to have aided his own passage over the Falls.

He had changed into his deck shoes, a pair of casual pants, a cardigan sweater and a watch cap at the marina. Now he stripped down to the pair of dark grey long johns. He didn't want to stand out in the night like a white rabbit, but in the event that he was unlucky enough to be rescued it would seem strange to be wearing camouflage gear and have waterproof black makeup smeared on his face.

He kept his deck shoes on. They were tightly laced and would be needed to scramble over the rocks.

He ripped the hook closure at the top of the pants to look as if he'd torn them off. Perhaps even in the water. He pulled sharply at the cardigan while keeping it buttoned. He was pleased to see one of the wooden buttons pop off and bounce across the deck. Probably none of his clothes would be found either, but if it was he wanted it to look convincing.

He had spent some time in the park on Goat Island and had, by observing flotsam carried along by the current, made an estimate of a point from which an object would be carried over unaided within 15 minutes. He doubted whether any police or emergency vehicle could be dispatched to the bank near the edge in anything less than 20 minutes. He didn't want anyone to observe that the boat was without passenger at that point.

Also, he intended his transmission to be so panicked and confused as to make it difficult for anyone to know where he was immediately.

He applied a little more power to the drive unit and steered stoically down river until he was approaching the point on the water at which action was required. He reached for his microphone and shouted into it in what he hoped would sound like confused panic: "Mayday. Mayday, Mayday, this is *Reflections*, *Reflections*, *Reflections*, my motor's out; I'm drifting toward the falls. Can anyone hear me?"

Almost immediately he got a response *"Reflections*, this is the U.S. Coast Guard. What is your position? What type of craft are you? Are you in immediate danger? Over."

Now was when he wanted to be as inefficient about his communication as possible. He punched the mike button and yelled into it. As long as he was talking they couldn't say anything to him or suggest any action which might help prevent his almost certain death as a result of being dragged over the brink. *"Reflections* to Coast guard. My motor's out. My motor's out. I'm drifting down river. I'm getting close to the Falls. I'm a 26 ft Chris Craft inboard/outboard, beige and brown. You should be able to see me on radar. My GPS is connected. Can you see me? Can you see me? Do you see where I am?" He knew he should say "over" but wanted them to think him completely panicked and out of control.

He released the button long enough to hear their response "Coast Guard to *Reflections*, negative on your position. How many persons on board? Do you have an MISS Button? Over."

"Yes! Yes!" he shouted. "I'm pushing it. I'm pushing it. It's only me on board. I have a life jacket." He did indeed have a very good personal flotation device. He had a Mustang self-inflating BC with a water contact activator. That device was presently lying on the rear bench seat of *Reflections* next to his cardigan and pants. Carl expected that it would be found floating below the Falls, mute proof to his futile attempt to survive.

At this point he did finally lift up the shield, push the alarm button, and wait the 5 seconds it took to activate.

His position would now be transmitted and they would realize how close he was to disaster. His propeller was still pushing him and giving him the ability to steer, although on their radar he must seem hopelessly far from shore. Gradually he edged a little closer to the Goat Island shoreline. The land appeared to be moving fairly rapidly by him. If he were concerned about dying he would certainly be alarmed at this point.

It wasn't that he didn't think he was going to die. The odds were that he would be dead ten minutes from now. He had a draw to a possible inside straight and one last card to come. Would he draw the card he needed? Probably not. If he filled the straight, would it win the hand? Unlikely. But he had everything riding on the slim chance that he would win. He was going all-in.

"My anchor broke loose. I can't stop. Should I try to swim to shore? What should I do? Can you get help to me or should I try to swim to shore?" Tell me not to try to swim, he hoped. I don't want them looking for me in the river.

"Do you have a back up anchor or grappling hook? Over."

Aha, they must realize that they can't get anyone here in time, but they don't want to take responsibility for sending me into the river which is equally futile.

"No, no, the line broke I think. I can see the edge of the Falls up ahead. Should I go into the water? Tell me what to do. I'll stay with the boat unless you think I should abandon ship."

He could indeed see the point where the river poured over and down into the chasm. As he had known they would be, the Falls were illuminated by huge light at this time of the evening. It would provide a real spectacle as *Reflections* took to the air. He wondered if anyone would catch it on video. Probably, even mobile phones could do that. He must be sure to get clear before someone caught him on camera.

That was why it was so important that he be off the boat and hidden on shore before anyone was on hand to see him.

He could picture the situation at the Coast Guard. They had someone on a radio, maybe a phone too, trying to get personnel to the water's edge, but they knew it was too late.

They knew if he stayed in the boat he was doomed, but how could they tell him to try to swim which was also hopeless? He actually felt guilty for what he was putting them through.

On the other hand, they were in a warm office; he was the one about to die.

While he had been talking to them, he had directed the boat as near to the bank as he could. The water was not deep here, but it was moving inexorably toward the drop off point. *Reflections* had a broad beam, but drew only about one foot of water. She would be swept over like a cork.

Now it was time to get ashore. But he did not want them to know he was going into the water so soon.

He ignored the radio. Let them imagine what was happening. He had told them that he would stay with the boat. He had to play his last card.

Chapter 68

On the River

When the fifth and final card is laid, it is called The River.

Carl was prepared to risk it all on a long shot.

As they used to say in the British comedy, Black Adder, he had a cunning plan.

He had a strong woven line tied around his waist with the best bow-line knot he could tie. The line was 80 feet long and the other end was attached to a five-pound grappling hook. He had practiced throwing the hook. On dry land, when he wasn't on an uneven deck which was already starting to move erratically, he could throw it about thirty feet.

The plan was that he would reach the trees along the shore with his throw. Then, in theory, one of the five points of the hook would snag in a tree, or bush, or some ground and hold tight. Then the 80 feet of line would swing him in close to shore.

Or… if the hook fell short, or failed to catch hold it would snag along the bottom of the river and he could struggle though the shallows over to the bank.

That was the plan.

Unfortunately he also remembered what Rocky used to say to Bullwinkle, "That trick never works."

If this were a movie, he would deploy a paraglider and soar off into the night. Unfortunately this was life and Carl was stuck with a hook and 80 feet of rope.

Reflections would be swept over the Falls. The fall, the rocks, and the pounding tons of water would reduce the hull to small pieces. The motor would probably be torn loose from the support beams and join the other non-buoyant debris at the bottom.

His body, if he went over too, would either be beaten into fish food or float down river in the circle of the current in the whirlpool gorge until someone hauled it out.

If, and this was a big if, he made it to shore, he would take his grapple and his scraped and bruised body and crawl into a culvert under a small bridge in the park.

The culvert was two feet wide and about forty feet long where it crossed under a walking path well back from the water. In it, he had hidden a sleeping bag and a green garbage bag with a clean change of clothes, some cash in U.S. dollars, and his driver's license and credit card in the name Cal Bridges. Carl had kept this alternate identification up to date and in good standing. Carl was careful.

He had made certain that neither the sleeping bag nor the document and clothes could be connected to Carl Hill.

If, as seemed more likely, he ended up at the bottom of Niagara Falls, the sleeping bag would eventually be found by a park employee or a squirrel. It would not be connected to the stupid idiot who went over the Falls in a boat.

If he did manage to get to the culvert unseen he would crawl into the khaki sleeping bag and remain there for at least 12 hours, perhaps until dark the next night. When the park was deserted again he would emerge, change into the fresh clothing, jam his old clothes, the hook and the rope into the sleeping bag, roll it up to look like a duffel bag, and walk out of the park.

He would check into a local motel for a few days. He had left his Spanish passport and Spanish identity cards at his mail drop stateside. He could take a taxi to it and pick up everything he needed to travel to Europe. A flight from Buffalo to Madrid or Malaga would be best.

Once in Europe he would disappear into the Costa del Sol like so many Ponzi artists and stockbrokers before him. With unemployment over thirty percent and the countryside filled with northern Europeans buying up all the old farmhouses and country villas, Spain was the perfect place to disappear. He would avoid his own property in Spain. There were lots of small towns north of Malaga where he could find accommodation.

However, all this might be considered long-term planning.

At the moment his problem was getting to shore.

He applied a bit more power to the engine and swerved toward the bank. A second later his inboard/outboard lower unit struck rock and tore itself apart.

Without hesitation Carl ran to the side of the boat nearest land and threw the grappling hook as hard as he could and hoped it would fasten onto something solid.

He couldn't wait to find out. As soon as the hook was soaring through the air, Carl threw himself overboard.

Chapter 69

New Players?

Normally, new players are not allowed to enter the game after it has commenced. It would put existing players at a disadvantage.

Unknown to Carl, the OPP, in response to "Snowy's" report had already contacted U.S. police and rescue units had been dispatched.

Long before Carl made his radio call to the Coast Guard, units were heading toward the Goat Island Park in hopes of throwing him a line. A helicopter would be airborne soon and an aerial approach would also be attempted.

From information received, dispatchers believed that they would be able to reach the area above the Falls in time to fire a safety line out into the water. There would be no attempt to save the boat. Priority would go to preserving lives.

The report had mentioned sighting one person on board, but they could not be sure there were not more passengers below deck.

They had established communications between the police dispatch and the U.S. Coast Guard. Even as they were speaking to the coast guard the radio call was being received from *Reflections*.

"How soon can you have people at the water's edge in the park?" Coast Guard Officer Sloan asked.

"We've dispatched all units in the area. ETA of the first unit is in about 5 minutes."

"That will be close," replied Sloan. "He's only about 15 minutes from there."

"We have a second unit on the way with a device to fire a life line. How many persons are on board?"

"Hold one moment." The police dispatcher could hear communication in the background. Then Sloan came back on the phone. "There is one person, I say again, one person on board."

That gives us a chance, thought the dispatcher. To the officer he said "He will have to get clear of the boat and try to swim in the other direction away from the Falls. That will give us separation between him and the boat. We can't fire the line until the boat goes past."

"Understood," said Sloan. "We'll relay that."

The dispatcher stayed on the phone while listening to radio traffic between squad cars and rescue unit vehicles. The first squad car was approaching the entrance to the park.

A few seconds later Sloan came back on the phone. "We've lost contact with the boater," he said. "We're trying to get through to him to tell him to abandon the boat, but he's not responding. We can't get a boat down into that section of the river. The only hope is to pluck him from the water."

"Do you have a positional fix on the boat?"

"Yes," Sloan responded. "It's just over 3,000 feet up river. We estimate water velocity at 14 knots. The boat will reach the Falls in about 4 minutes."

There's not enough time, thought the dispatcher.

He placed a call to the squad car, Able Nine, and told the officers they would have to try to do something without waiting for the rescue unit. "The boat might be there in 3 to 4 minutes."

"He may not be with the boat. He may be in the water and trying to reach shore. Watch for him. You may be able to stick out something for him to grab. If you have a rope, try tying it to a nightstick to throw."

"Roger that. We're just coming in sight of the water."

"Stay at least 100 yards or so above the edge," he told them. "The current gets too fast after that."

The dispatcher heard nothing from the squad car for a little over one minute. In the meantime the rescue unit reported arriving at the park entrance. They had monitored the radio traffic with the squad car and were going to head straight to the bank.

Two minutes later, squad car Charlie Two called in to relay news. They informed dispatch that the boat had gone over the edge.

A few minutes later dispatch received a transmission from the first officers on the scene. "Dispatch, this is Able Nine. The boat drifted right by here just as we arrived. We've been watching the river and checking the bank, but there's no one. We're currently working upstream along the water's edge. Over."

"Roger that, Able Nine. More units are on the way. Over."

Chapter 70

All-in

The act of going All-in, betting all one's chips, is a crucial and potentially dangerous act. A player doing so risks losing everything.

When he hit the water, all was confusion. The shock of the cold water and the tumbling of the current completely disoriented him.

The water was not deep. He was aware of bumping against the bottom as he was carried along by the current. Seconds later the rope went taut and he felt the water sweeping around him.

He felt as if he was being dragged through the water like a fish on a line. Unlike a fish, he couldn't breathe under water. With one hand on the rope that stretched out in front of him he struggled to get his head above water. He broke the surface briefly and gasped in some air.

This was not good. He had to try to get to shore. The hook was caught on something, but he couldn't tell if it was on shore or in the river.

He was afraid to pull on the line too much for fear of dislodging it. Finally he got himself partially upright and saw the shore off to his left. He pushed as best he could on the bottom of the river. The rocks were smooth and slippery, but he was scrambling ever closer to the bank.

Just as he reached out to grab at some branches which hung out over the water, the rope went slack and he slipped.

Chapter 71

Spectators

Although spectators are allowed, they do not usually affect the game.

The night was chilly enough that the clients at the Table Rock restaurant were not dining on the terrace which overlooked the cascading water across the gorge. All were taking their meals inside. A few had come out from their tables inside to take photos of the Falls lit up by the bank of large spotlights.

The colours changed in regular progression and the tourists snapped away with digital cameras. At least half of them had not turned off the flash features on their cameras, so their photos would come out dark and out of focus.

At some point one of the photographers noticed a white object on the water above the Falls. He pointed at it and voices were raised in a mixture of excitement and consternation. Was this part of the show? What was that? It looked like a boat.

As they watched, the boat neared the edge, then seeming to pause for an instant, tumbled over and fell toward the dark water below.

Within seconds their cries had brought dozens of other diners and even waiters rushing out onto the terrace.

By the time two minutes had elapsed they were telling each other what they had seen. Several had been the first to spot the boat as it approached. At least twenty had seen it come shooting over the edge. Some had even seen bodies tossed from it as it fell. One elderly gentleman from Idaho had counted five separate individuals flailing out as they fell toward certain death.

Slightly enhanced versions of their testimony would appear in local newspapers in the following days. A front-page article in The Niagara Falls Review would feature a photograph of the gentleman from Idaho pointing at the place on the Falls where he had seen the boat come over the brink.

No bodies had been recovered, but many of the witnesses were certain they had seen at least one person swept over with, or near, the boat.

Chapter 72

Game Over

A tournament game continues until one of two things occurs. Either one player has all the chips or all remaining players have agreed to quit and divide the winnings.

The police and rescue crews searched every foot of the shoreline and shone spotlights back and forth across the water. The river was very shallow in spots and before now individuals swept down river had been rescued as they clung to a bit of rocky shoal.

They found nothing to indicate anyone had survived.

Down in the gorge, boat cushions and broken sections of the boat floated down river or were sucked back to be pushed under and ripped apart by the immense power of the water. Lights had picked out a brightly coloured personal flotation device, but there had been no sign of a person floating or swimming in the water.

A search and rescue crew stood by with a Zodiac. Hundreds of eyes scanned the water above and below the Falls. A police helicopter hovered over Goat Island with bright lights illuminating it in case someone had managed to scramble onto it.

It was certainly possible to go over the Falls and survive. Though many had died attempting to do so in sealed containers of various types, before it was made illegal, some had lived. There had been the miraculous case of a young boy who had gone over in a life jacket in the 1950's and been plucked unharmed from the swirling currents.

The recovery of his body was by no means certain. In October of 1995 a person with the unlikely name of Robert Overcracker had gone over the falls on a jetski. Although he had been seen falling in the air his body had never been recovered.

Carl would not be the first person named 'Hill' to have gone into the Niagara River. William "Red" Hill floated down the lower rapids in a six foot long steel barrel from the Maid of the Mist landing dock below the Falls at Queenston in 1930.

As time passed, hopes that this boater had escaped dimmed.

Crowds grew and the number of people who had seen, or heard, or 'expected something like this to happen' increased with time.

Chapter 73

Results are posted

In a very large tournament the order of finish will be posted.

Joyce had retired to read in bed when the telephone rang.

She was used to the fact that clients often made calls at all hours. They would suddenly need to know something about a listed property which they had to know now instead of during the next day's business hours. It went with the job.

Setting her book aside, she put the receiver to her ear and said hello.

"Mrs. Hill?" a male voice asked.

"Yes. How may I help you?" she replied with her professional voice.

"This is Niagara Regional Police. Is your husband at home?" the voice continued.

"No, he's at a friend's house. Why? Is something wrong?" Joyce demanded.

"We're investigating an occurrence. Do you or your husband own a boat?"

"Yes. We have a boat at the Chippawa Marina. Has there been some damage to the boat?" Joyce asked. It was annoying

how police seemed always to avoid giving out information.
They just keep asking questions.

"There is a police officer on his way to your home now. He
can fill you in," the Voice annoyed her by replying.

Joyce knew there was no use in asking for information from
this official, so she hung up the phone and put on her newest
housecoat. As she made her way downstairs, she decided to call
Carl at the poker game. It was at Tom's tonight, she recalled
him saying.

She picked up the hall phone and used the speed dial to place
a call. After a few rings, Tom picked up.

"Hi Tom. Sorry to disturb the game. Could I speak with
Carl please?" she asked.

"Carl's not here right now. He said he had to do something
at the boat. He should be back here soon," Tom surprised her by
responding.

"Please have him call me right away when he gets back," she
asked. Joyce was starting to get worried. Had something
happened?

The doorbell rang as she was setting down the phone and she
hurried over to the door. A uniformed police officer was on the
porch.

"Mrs. Hill?" the officer asked as she opened the door.

"Yes. Has something happened?" She was now quite
alarmed.

"I'm sorry. There's been a boating accident. Could I ask
you a few questions please?"

The rest of the night was a nightmare of reassurances that all
that could be done to find Carl was being done. She was

cautioned to try to remain calm. Tom's wife, Sharon, called her and then insisted on coming over to be with her.

After the officer left, Sharon and Joyce sat together in the kitchen and time seemed both stretched and twisted.

Joyce made a number of calls which only made her more uncertain. Finally she made up the spare bed for Sharon and she lay down on the couch in her housecoat.

Joyce woke with a start to find Sharon in the room with her hand on Joyce's shoulder. The autumn sunshine was flooding into the room.

"There's a police officer here," Sharon told her.

Joyce removed the cover Sharon must have put on her. She got up and pulled her housecoat into place as she walked out to the hall where the officer waited.

"Have you found him?" she asked, fearing the worst.

"Not yet," answered the officer. "His car has been found at the marina. I could drive someone up there to pick it up if you like."

"Why would he have gone out on the river?" Joyce demanded. "It doesn't make sense."

"We're not sure," the officer replied shaking his head. "But, he was seen on the river in the boat by an OPP officer and he made a distress call to the U.S. Coast Guard."

"Let me get dressed and I'm coming with you to the car," Joyce heard herself say.

She turned and climbed the stairs. This can't be, she thought. How can this be?

Chapter 74

Under the Gun

The player to the left of the Big Blind is first to make a decision whether to play or drop out. This position and decision are called "Under the Gun."

The next few days were a blur. She phoned into work and had someone take over her open house and office duties. She went over the past few days in search of some clue in something he may have said to indicate that Carl was despondent or worried.

She couldn't think of anything specific. He had seemed happy if anything. She didn't think Carl would even contemplate suicide. Besides he would have said something or left her a note.

Then Thursday morning, Sam Gampton called.

Sam was a lawyer who had drawn up their wills and who Carl seemed to like. He didn't like lawyers in general, but Sam seemed to appeal to Carl's sense of humour.

"Joyce," Sam said. "I wonder if you could come by my office today or tomorrow. I've got something to give you."

"From Carl?" Joyce guessed.

"Yes," Sam said. "From Carl."

"I'm coming right now," she said.

Chapter 75

Dead Man's Hand

Legend has it that Wild Bill Hickok was shot in the back while playing poker. The cards he held in his hand were two pair: Aces and Eights. His first mistake was sitting with his back to the door.

Sam had a small private practice in an older building. He had been there for many years and his secretary had been with him forever. Sam didn't look like a prosperous lawyer, and he did look as if he cared. Sam was an old time socialist from the times when the young believed they could make a better world.

Seated behind his old oak desk, files of papers lining the walls along with an assortment of well used law books, Sam resembled an owl. He had large intelligent eyes and his old-fashioned large glasses accentuated them. Even his clothing seemed somewhat feathery.

He must have had this pointed out to him at some time in his career, because various figural carvings of owls were on his desks and perched on shelves behind him.

Sam did not look like an owl of prey; rather he reminded Joyce of the fussy and slightly bewildered owl of the original drawings in Winnie the Pooh. The owl who could spell his name Wol and who invited Pooh and Piglet for tea.

Alarmed as she felt, Joyce was still pleased to see Sam. He was a reassuring figure.

Sam was well into his 60s but showed no sign that he ever intended to retire. Joyce realized that she didn't know if Sam was married and wondered about his relationship with his secretary.

"Come in, Joyce," Sam called out as soon as he saw her from his office doorway. "I'm sorry to hear about the boat accident. Please have a seat."

Joyce settled into the big oak client chair and looked Sam in the eyes. "Did Carl kill himself?" she asked and watched closely to judge his reaction to the question.

Sam seemed genuinely puzzled. "I would be surprised if that were so, but I'm not sure," he replied. "He came to see me Monday with a package which he asked me to give to you after Wednesday."

"Did he say why, or explain?" she queried.

"No. He just said he wanted to make sure it was kept safe and delivered into your hands in case something happened to him. I have no idea what is inside."

Sam took a small package out of his desk and handed it to Joyce.

Joyce took the package and opened it. There was nothing inside except a computer disc.

The disc looked like many they had at home. Carl used discs which looked like this one to download movies from their video camera.

There was no note, just a label on the disc that read: "Joyce, please watch this alone."

"One other thing I should mention, Joyce," Sam said in his gentle way. "I looked over your wills. Almost everything you own is in joint ownership or goes to you on his death, including your bank accounts. You need do nothing at once. Even Carl's car registration can be left alone for now."

"Thank you, Sam. I'll be in touch if I need anything."

"Please do call if I can do anything at all," Sam said as he walked her out through his outer office area.

Chapter 76

Pass to the Power

In the progress of betting each hand one player may demonstrate confidence by betting heavily. Other players may, half mockingly say "Pass to the power" rather than betting in their turn.

Joyce drove home faster than Carl would have recommended.

She went directly to Carl's office, turned on his computer, and put in the disc. Somehow it seemed appropriate to watch it in his office.

The video started with Carl looking into the camera. His first words were: *"I'm sorry. If I could find any other way out I wouldn't put you through this. As you watch this I may be dead. If I am dead they may have found my body and you will know that I am dead. If they did not find my body there is a chance that I am alive. Please understand that I love you. I have been forced to do what I am doing because of a very real threat from my past which could destroy us both if I did nothing. I know what you have just gone through and are still going through is horrible. If I am alive, I will send you an e-mail. I will send an e-mail as soon as I can, but it may take several days. If I am*

dead, please believe that what I have done was to try to save us.
If I am alive you must let no one know, no one at all. There is
an envelope with some money in the top drawer of my desk. I
love you more than ever at this moment. I hope I will see you
again."

The screen went blank.

Joyce immediately went to the internet connection and
opened her e-mail.

Joyce had to put her password in twice to get it right. Be
calm, even if he's alive he may not have sent anything yet, she
thought.

Then she had another thought: if he's alive, I'll kill him.

When her mail opened she scanned quickly down through
the spam and offers of a penis enlargement until she found one
from Carl's e-mail address. It was dated today.

She clicked to open the e-mail and then had to stop to wipe
her eyes so she could read it. She was suddenly sobbing and
tears were pouring out of her eyes so hard she could hardly see.

Chapter 77

A player asks for time

A limited quota of extra time can be granted to a player who requests more time to make a decision.

There was a message from Carl.

Dear Joyce,

I am alive and I hope that you will forgive me. Please give me a chance to explain. You must continue to pretend that you think that I am dead. I want to give you time to think everything through. Then if you are willing to meet me I will explain everything and keep no secret from you.

It is not safe for me to remain in North America. I will get to Europe somehow, though I do not yet know the route I will take.

If you are willing to meet with me and hear my reasons for what I have done we can meet in Spain. The money in the desk drawer is enough to pay for a trip to Europe. For security reasons I recommend that you go to England first. You have relatives there and it will seem reasonable for you to go there.

For reasons I will explain later I ask that you do not go to England for another three weeks. Send me an e-mail at this address with your phone number when you are in England. I will phone you and we can arrange a meeting place in Spain.

Perhaps you have already decided to write me off. I hope not. I will monitor this e-mail address but dare not use it again to send.

Love, Carl.

Joyce read through the note three times. It was clear enough, but she could not imagine what made it necessary.

She walked out to the kitchen and poured herself a glass of water.

From the living room she looked out at the trees across the river. The leaves were changing colour. Some were even falling from the trees. Winter was coming.

She walked back into Carl's office, opened the drawer and found the envelope.

There was a lot of money in the envelope.

Joyce thought for a moment. Then she sent a reply to Carl's e-mail.

Carl,

I love you too. I will come to you. It had better be a good reason.

Love, Joyce.

Chapter 78

Trap bet; Check and Raise

A player with a strong hand may pretend weakness by checking and then after another player has committed himself by a large bet, the original player will make a big raise or even go all-in.

The downtown Malaga internet café was almost empty during the afternoon quiet period when most sensible Spaniards take at least two hours away from work. The screen in front of Carl, known to most people locally as Carlo, showed a section of the Buffalo Gazette from Oct 4.

Under the headline: **Suspected Gang Member found Dead** was a report that made it clear that Ronnie was history.

A middle aged male, identified as Cameron "Ronnie" Alistair MacKenzie, was found bludgeoned to death.

A local proprietor made a grisly discovery shortly after closing down in the early hours of Sunday, Oct. 3

The body was found lying in the parking lot of the Brickyard tavern in downtown Lewiston. Robbery is suspected since the deceased had recently been seen flashing a lot of money about and no money was found on the body.

Though presently employed as a chauffeur by a local businessman, the victim had a prior criminal record. Police are pursuing a number of leads.

That would be Ronnie, Carl thought. Ronnie had chosen to be known as "Ronnie" for similar reasons Wolf had for avoiding Wolfgang. He could have been "Al" but there were already several fellows named Al in the neighbourhood.

Now, how could Ronnie have ended up dead?

Oh, I know, thought Carl. It's probably because of the contract I took out on him through Stan when I called from Buffalo. Stan was pleased to help out and had given him a professional discount price of $50,000.

It was a shame he had had to waste another $10,000 in cash to temporarily divert Ronnie, but at least it made for a good reason for authorities to suspect that that was the reason he was killed.

Carl believed that his own presumed death would have been sufficient to put Ronnie off his trail. But why take chances?

Chapter 79

Show Down

After two or more players have stayed in up until the final bet, they turn up their cards in a Show Down. Literally "Show what you have down."

The sky was blue; the air was clear; the sun was bright and warm. Carl was sitting on the private terrace of a small hotel and restaurant, El Molino de los Abuelos, in the mountains north of Malaga.

Joyce was coming today.

In the distance he could see the blue waters of the Mediterranean.

This morning she was flying into Malaga from Heathrow.

The town, Comares, was not far from the sea or from Malaga, but the mountain roads were steep and winding. It would take her taxi an hour to bring her here from the airport.

Carl had considered meeting her plane, but had decided that it was best to see her again, for the first, and perhaps the last time, here in this hilltop town surrounded by mountains and nature.

He looked at his watch again. Her plane had landed. She would be getting into a taxi in a few minutes. She would soon be here.

Here they could talk without the distractions of quotidian life.

He would tell her everything. If they were to be together, it must be without secrets.

He had been at this hotel for almost a week. For tonight he had rented a second room in case Joyce wanted to stay to think things over without sharing his bed.

They had met in Cuba almost 25 years ago. Today would decide whether they would continue together.

Carl: one; River: zero

His gamble had paid off.

His grappling hook had caught in the edge of the bank. He struggled over to it and onto the shore. The hook and rope came with him into the culvert. He crawled to his bundle halfway through the tunnel of darkness. He was cold and wet, but unharmed except far a few scrapes.

Once inside the sleeping bag he pulled the top down so that even a flashlight shone into the culvert would reveal only a bundle of rags. He listened intently for sounds of searchers.

No one came near the roadway where it crossed the small dry creek. Why would they? They were looking for someone seeking to be rescued, not someone trying to hide.

The next day there was the distant sound of vehicles from time to time and Carl, true to his nature, decided to play it safe and wait for the next period of darkness.

Twenty-four hours in a damp sleeping bag, in a culvert, in September, is less interesting than it might be supposed.

On top of everything else, Carl had to pee.

During the early hours of the morning he carefully turned face down and opened the zipper of the sleeping bag. By raising himself onto his knees and pressing his forehead down onto the ground he managed to raise himself enough to pee into a depression he scratched in the debris at the bottom of the culvert.

He covered it up like a cat and tried to roll over to drag the edge of the bag over the spot.

Although he had been desperate to relieve himself he found that he did not feel much better afterwards.

When he finally crawled out of the culvert it was just past midnight, a little more than one day after he had entered it.

The park was deserted. He dressed himself in the clean clothes which he had in a green garbage bag and put his old, still wet clothes into it instead. He rolled the grappling hook and the garbage bag inside the sleeping bag and used the length of rope to tie to up like a bed roll.

He walked out of the park without being seen and went to a small tourist motel. Night clerks at motels don't worry too much as long as you have identification, a credit card, and pay cash in advance. He probably looked no worse than many who turn up after midnight looking for a room.

The next day he took a taxi downtown to a clothing store and bought some casual clothing and a small suitcase. His next stop was to pick up his Spanish passport and some more cash from the mail drop. Then he checked into a slightly more upscale hotel in downtown Buffalo and got rid of the bed roll in a dumpster.

He read a few newspapers and decided that the reports of his death had met his expectations. He sent an e-mail to Joyce Thursday morning and Thursday evening received her reply. He would not risk using that e-mail address again until he was in Europe.

Three days later he was on a flight to Spain.

Carl was standing at the front of the hotel when Joyce's taxi arrived.

He paid the driver.

Then he took Joyce in his arms and said "Thank you for coming."

Joyce looked him in the eyes and said "So, who did you kill?"

Carl took her hand and as they walked through the hotel lobby to the terrace he answered, "It's a long story. Perhaps we should sit down to discuss it."

About the Author

E. Craig McKay was city born and bred. He could hotwire a car and fashion a switchblade before reaching grade 7. Summers were spent in northern Ontario where he learned to love boating and water sports. He worked on the docks of Toronto's waterfront and drove taxi and beer truck before graduating with an undergraduate degree in Philosophy and a Masters of Arts, English. Post graduate studies in Quebec City, Canada and University of Nice, France led to his appreciation of good food and fine wine. He launched a wine importation company in 1984 and has travelled yearly to Europe for more than twenty-five years. Although an active international pistol and shotgun competitor, he has never accidently shot anyone nor been convicted of a major crime.

Did you enjoy Hit by the Dealer?

Look for the next book in the series, Cross Country Hit, in September of 2012.

Learn about another of Stan's agents as Hall Brothers Entertainment proudly publishes the fantastic follow-up to Hit by the Dealer.